His Red Eyes Again

His Red Eyes Again

Edited by
Julia Kruk and Tracy Lee

Published in the UK in 2013 by The Dracula Society
www.thedraculasociety.org.uk

Cover Design © Berni Stevens
http://bernistevensdesign.com
Typesetting by Tracy Lee

ISBN: 978-1491049617

British Library Cataloguing in Publication Data.
A catalogue record for this book is available from the British Library.

'The setting sun, low down in the sky, was just dropping behind Kettleness. The red light was thrown over on the East Cliff and the old abbey, and seemed to bathe everything in a beautiful rosy glow. We were silent for a while, and suddenly Lucy murmured as if to herself . . . 'His red eyes again! They are just the same.' It was such an odd expression, coming apropos of nothing, that it quite startled me. I slewed round a little, so as to see Lucy well without seeming to stare at her, and saw that she was in a half dreamy state, with an odd look on her face that I could not quite make out, so I said nothing, but followed her eyes. She appeared to be looking over at our own seat, whereon was a dark figure seated alone. I was quite a little startled myself, for it seemed for an instant as if the stranger had great eyes like burning flames.'

Mina Murray's Journal, August 14th
From *Dracula* by Bram Stoker

This book is dedicated to the memory of
Bernard Davies and Bruce Wightman,
the founders of the Dracula Society

CONTENTS

FOREWORD

You are holding in your hands something of which the Dracula Society can be very proud.

Ten years ago, to mark our 30th anniversary, those of us on Committee at the time thought it would be a great idea to produce an anthology of vampire stories, written by Society members, to be launched at our Convention in Rochester over the Halloween weekend of 2003. *Conventional Vampires* contained nine stories, and some vampire verses by its editor, Tina Rath. The stories were good, and the front cover boasted an excellent piece of artwork by Ken Barr. But publishing options for such a relatively small print run were far more limited then than is the case today. Now, to commemorate the Dracula Society's 40th anniversary, we are able to present you with a proper book, complete with spine, ISBN, excellent cover design, and at an affordable price.

His Red Eyes Again opens with a very special guest contribution from bestselling author, Chris Priestley. I have long been a huge admirer of both Chris's children's and young adult novels – probably because he is so obviously inspired by the same great gothic/horror writers that *I* love. Chris deservedly won the Dracula Society's Children of the Night Award in 2009 for *Tales of Terror from the Tunnel's Mouth,* and now he has written a Victorian vampire tale especially for our 40th anniversary anthology.

Of the remaining twelve stories, six are by members who contributed to our original *Conventional Vampires.* Old world Romania clashes with modern day London in Sue Gedge's wry take on what it means to be a vampire, and Katherine Haynes leads us right into the 'land beyond the forest' for her traditional vampire tale with a modern twist. Barry McCann sets his story in a remote Cornish village sometime after the Great War. Rosemary Laurey, by contrast, creates a futuristic modern US urban setting for her tale of vampires and bounty hunters, while Berni Stevens takes us back to a grim Victorian London. And instead of a poem entitled 'Fluffy', Tina Rath, the last of those original contributors a decade ago, has come up with a very funny tale called 'Scruffy'. Humour predominates again in both Gail-Nina Anderson's tale of selling the supernatural on eBay, and Tony Lee's take on those imaginary friends of childhood; and we stay in contemporary mode in Laura Miller's story of vampires entering the life of a fashion-conscious London socialite. Alan Brown then returns us to familiar Gothic literary vampire territory, while both Jason D. Brawn and Anna Taborska go straight for the jugular in their nightmarishly creepy vampire tales.

We hope you enjoy this collection. There really is something here for everyone: chills, humour, wit, and occasional quirkiness. I would like to thank my fellow co-editor, Tracy Lee, for her meticulous editing and for all her help in getting the anthology together, and also Berni Stevens for her moody Gothic cover design.

Why 'His Red Eyes Again'? Readers familiar with Bram Stoker's original groundbreaking vampire novel will immediately recognise the reference, and to whom those eyes belong. And if you have come across this volume but have not yet encountered the Dracula Society, then do have a look at our website. It is true that we are London-based, and that our meetings are held in London; but we do travel – in search of *Dracula* in Transylvania, *Nosferatu* in Slovakia, the *Phantom of the Opera* and Grand Guignol in Paris, even mummies in Egypt. And there are enough ghosts and witches and other literary haunts to explore closer to home. So we're not just about *Dracula*. Perhaps you'd like to join us.

Julia Kruk
Chair and Treasurer
The Dracula Society
www.thedraculasociety.org.uk

MRS BENSON
Chris Priestley

Some years ago I was entrusted by Charles F___ of San Francisco with the task of archiving the papers of his family. They were extraordinarily wealthy and powerful. They had paid for the building of a new library wing at the university and wanted their papers to form part of a larger archive of material concerned with the early years of the city. I was only a few years out of university myself, and was surprised, but delighted to be asked.

I worked in the very fine library in their house overlooking the bay. I had been working on the papers for about a month, slowly and methodically going through a box file containing a fascinating confusion of letters, bills of sale and newspaper cuttings, when I came across a number of pages that I surmised to have been ripped from a journal (though I never did discover that journal, if indeed it still existed).

The pages were not dated, nor were they signed, but I recognised the hand immediately as that of Henry F___, my employer's father and founder of the dynasty. But nothing I had read thus far by Henry could possibly have prepared me for the contents of these particular pages.

Once I had read through them, and then read through them again, I took them straight to my employer. We had previously agreed that I should not bother him until the entire archive was collated, but I felt that he should be informed immediately of what must surely be the most extraordinary discovery the archive was likely to reveal.

Charles F___ was not a man I warmed to. He had the business man's distrust of the academic. He had little intellectual enthusiasm and cared little for the library wing that would bear his family's name save, I believe, for the mark it would make in the society he wished, for business purposes, to court.

I watched him read the pages, astonished at how little reaction he showed to its contents. He could have been reading an invoice or a letter from his mother. He read slowly and when he had finally finished, he got up without saying a word and walked over to the fireplace where he leaned over and held out the papers above the flames dancing in the hearth.

I leapt to my feet and called to him to stop, and he turned, his expression revealing, I think, the fact no one had ever said this to him before in his entire life. He stared at me in disbelief, a wry smile on his face. I asked him what he was doing.

F___ explained to me in very few words and with some impatience that he could not allow what must clearly be the signs of some mental laxity or evidence of drinking or worse to be preserved in the family archive for the amusement of, as he put it, 'so-called scholars'.

Even if he felt that way, I protested, riled by these last words of his, then surely he could at least preserve the papers in some private family archive where it might be accessible at a much later date when none could be harmed by it. He shook his head and turned towards the fire.

I told him outright that what he was contemplating was an outrage and that if he committed those papers to the flames then I could not in all conscience continue in his employment and that he would have to find another to complete my work.

'Very well,' he said. 'As you wish.' And then he dropped the papers into the fire.

I must have had some suspicion that this might be my employer's reaction. In any event, when I packed my bag and left that house for the last time, I carried with me a fair copy of the journal pages, which I had carefully made before showing the original to F___.

It was of course an appalling contravention of my duty of confidentiality towards my employer, and I had never before been guilty of such a thing. Neither have I ever felt compelled to repeat that crime.

I suppose that I felt the contents of the pages to be too strange - too extraordinary, too clearly of great interest - to be obliterated in that fashion, simply to spare F___ personal embarrassment. Having said that, I was naturally unable to publish the extract because F___ would surely have seen to it that my reputation was destroyed, something of which he was well-placed to do.

And so I have consigned these pages to my own papers and entrusted them to my lawyers for some future version of myself to discover and be likewise startled and amazed. If I am addressing that person now, then welcome, fellow traveller, and read on.

I need only add that though the extract was not dated it seems to have been written during the 1880s, when Henry F___ was travelling extensively in the Old West, building the empire of hardware shops that would become the basis of the huge business empire he would command in his later years. That period provided a great many fascinating insights into our country's history. But nothing quite like what is to follow. I will let Henry continue in his own words . . .

I must set down the events of the last hours and days immediately. If I wait too long I will begin to doubt my memory, or even my own faculties. Certainly those who may one day read this may doubt both. All I can say is that what you read here is the truth. Good Lord, look how my hand shakes as I write!

I am sitting in the wilfully misnamed Grand Hotel in Abraham. It is late - or perhaps, more properly, it is very early. Dawn is breaking and I have not slept. The westbound Frisco train will soon be here, but it will leave without me. She - and he - will board, but not I. I will not go another mile in their company - not for all the money in the world.

They are in a room just down the hall. That fact alone may account for my inability to sleep and

I confess that I have checked the lock on my door at least four times. You are impatient to learn, of course, why a grown man should fear a woman and child, but have a little patience: it is a short tale.

I met them in the flea-bitten town of Blind Creek, Missouri. I was travelling through, signing up hardware stores to my company. It has been a good trip, if exhausting. I have managed to convince a good many storekeepers of the value of having my expertise, my financing and my distribution (though all of those things are as yet a good deal more vague than I was willing to let on). All going well, I think I may finally be on the way to making something of myself. I was itching to get the railroad back to San Francisco and take stock, but I dare say one day won't make any great difference to my fortunes. But I digress. Back to the subjects of my tale . . .

As I walked towards the Wells Fargo office to buy a seat on the next stage bound for Abraham, from whence I would catch my train, I saw the kind of disgraceful scene that is sadly all too common in these wilder parts.

It was dusk. A young lady was trying to make her way along the boardwalk - a mother and a small child to make matters worse - and she was being obstructed by a group of the low sort of drunks and drifters who frequent the saloons and bars thereabouts.

Though it was barely five in the evening the smell of cheap whisky was all too detectable from twenty yards away. I could hear them making the most obscene remarks to the lady in question and I decided that I must, as a Christian, intervene on her behalf.

I would like to think that I am no coward (though what man is a true judge of his own bravery?) but I have seen with my own eyes what befalls a man who seeks a confrontation with men such as these. There was no mileage in inflaming the situation. Instead, I ambled forward bashfully and pretended to be the lady's husband, saying, 'Ah there you are dear, I was wondering where you were' and such like.

I did my best not to make eye contact with any of the men and after a few taunting remarks directed at me, to which I knew better than to respond, they let us continue on our way.

Once we were a safe distance away, the lady thanked me for coming to her assistance and I apologised for taking the liberty of pretending intimacy with her. She smiled and assured me that no offence was taken. We were standing in the amber glow of a nearby window and I saw for the first time how beautiful she was.

Her beauty was of a fragile kind though. She was clearly not in good health. Her face was pale and drawn. She had a deep red scarf at her throat and that only served to make her pallor seem all the more pronounced.

Despite the decrepit surroundings, they were both dressed as though they were about to take a stroll in a city park on a chill September evening. The little boy wore a wide brimmed hat that struggled to stay on his head as he pressed his face into his mother's skirts. I took him to be bashful or understandably upset by the behaviour of the men.

The lady took my hand and thanked me again. Her own hand was gloved and surprisingly cold. I noticed too that there were several small bloodstains on the pale leather and I suspected that her looks might be explained by consumption. I asked her if I could be of any further assistance and offered to at least walk her and her son to their destination so as to avoid any similar mishaps.

She smiled and said that would not be necessary. She was staying at the hotel across the street and she was catching the next stagecoach out of town the following morning. I said that I myself was staying at that very hotel travelling on that same stagecoach. I told her that I would see her to the hotel and in the morning - if she was agreeable - I would escort her to the staging post.

She did agree, and the three of us checked out together. The stagecoach was full at the point of departure. Our fellow passengers were all of one group: men of different ages from the same family, all of them bound for the funeral of a relative who owned a large ranch an hour or two out of town. Despite - or maybe because of - the sadness of their journey, two of the younger men tried their best to engage with the little boy, but the little fellow ignored their advances and tucked himself tightly into his mother, never once looking out. I was still yet to have a clear view of the boy's face. A melancholy silence settled on the carriage.

The men eventually alighted at a windswept point on the road at a junction with a track that snaked off into the distance. A wagon was there to meet them and they said their goodbyes to us, before climbing aboard. Soon we were on our way again, and the wagon and the men were erased by a cloud of dust.

I was alone once more with the lady and her

son. She had barely spoken a word the entire journey. I put that down to a not surprising feeling of modesty, finding herself in a crowded carriage of strange men. But she was just as taciturn now those men had departed. All my attempts at conversation were greeted with politeness but little enthusiasm.

After several hours I had learned little about her save for the fact that her name was Mrs Benson, that she was a widow, had lived most her life in Jackson, Mississippi and was bound - as I was - for the town of Abraham and thence to San Francisco. She gave me no reason as to why she was leaving Jackson, or what she hoped to find in Frisco.

Our journey was delayed for some time whilst the driver made some running repairs to the back axle, which had seemingly been damaged by a stone thrown up by the wheels. We were not so very far from our destination, but as the daylight began to fade in the west, I could see the guard hug his shotgun a little tighter and peer off into the scrub. Mrs Benson took her son a little way off to answer the call of nature.

When she returned, looking paler than ever in the dim light, she staggered and almost fell down in a faint - would have fallen, had I not reached out to catch her. The driver said we had better be moving on and I helped Mrs Benson into the carriage.

I was mightily relieved when the wheels began to turn and pick up speed. She asked if I would mind if we closed the window curtains. She said that her son was tired and it might help him to sleep. I naturally agreed, though I felt sure the need for sleep was more hers than his, and we continued on our way.

The boy was now sitting on his mother's lap. I was a little surprised by this as he seemed a little old for that kind of thing, but I did not pay it further heed as I simply put it down to fatigue and the stress of travelling. The boy nuzzled his face into his mother's neck so that his head obscured her throat, and she closed her eyes and fell asleep, her lips slightly parted, her breathing shallow.

I watched her in the gathering gloom for a while before my own eyelids began to feel heavy and I drifted into sleep myself. I cannot say how long I slept, but I was jolted awake suddenly. The carriage was much darker now and it took a little while to discern anything in the gloom. I pulled the curtain beside me aside and peered out. I could see that we were approaching the outskirts of Abraham and I was glad of it.

It was then that my ears began to pick out a sound - to pick it clear of the rumble of the wheels and the creak and clatter of the carriage and the drumming of the horses' hooves. It was a quiet sound, but a disturbing one. It sounded like the lapping of a cat.

And it was coming from inside the carriage.

My eyes took a little while to adjust to the gloom. I saw that instead of sitting, the boy was now kneeling on his mother's lap, a position that was surely uncomfortable to her, and indeed I saw by her face that she did seem to be in some pain. The boy's head obscured her throat and was moving in time to the sound of lapping.

I was overcome with some kind of instinctive fear. It was all I could do to stop myself opening the carriage door and hurling myself out. I cried out and the boy turned to me. Or should I say he turned on *me!*

He hissed like a cat, his lips pulled back to reveal two sharp teeth smeared with blood. The lower part of his face was likewise smeared with blood. I reached into my coat for my pistol as the boy leaned towards me but his mother pulled him back and pushed herself between us. Her white collar was open and her blouse unbuttoned to reveal a bloody wound in her pale flesh. She saw where my eyes fell and quickly buttoned her blouse and replaced the red scarf (the reason for which was now clear).

I had pressed myself against the opposite side of the carriage and made sure I could always keep in view that boy-shaped fiend. He peeped out from behind her horribly as she took a small towel from her bag and cleaned his face.

'What is that . . . thing?' I asked when I was finally able to speak.

'He is my son!' she said, as though this ended the matter.

'Your son?' I said, looking at the boy in disgust. 'He is some kind of monster!'

'He is my - son!' she repeated vehemently. 'It is not his fault he is . . . the way he is. He is the victim of a disease.'

'Is that what you call it?' I said. 'A disease?'

'It is an infection,' she said. 'Is a person who catches smallpox at fault?' Should they be punished?'

'But . . . how . . .

'The governess I employed to look after him. How she contracted the disease I know not . . .'

'Was she apprehended, this governess?' I asked.

She shook her head wearily.

'After passing on the evil to my son, she fled and I never saw her again.'

'And are you . . . have you . . . ?'

'No,' she said. "The governess pricked her finger whilst sewing one day and my little boy kissed it better. I think she was already infected and that is how it is passed.'

I saw tears sparkle in her eyes.

'I will nurture him for as long as I am able,' she said. 'As any mother would.'

'And when he kills you?' I said. 'As he surely will. What then?'

She did not - could not - answer. We sat in silence for a while, the boy eyeing me suspiciously all the while. Whether he feared me I could not say, but I found myself putting my hand to my throat and was relieved to find that it was untouched.

We were arriving in Abraham. I could see the panic growing in her face. She feared what I planned to do when the stagecoach came to a halt. My disgust for the son was balanced by a great sympathy for the mother. Perhaps if she had not been so beautiful . . .

I let them go. What could I do? Tell the town sheriff that there was a boy in his town - a boy who was a . . . I cannot even now bring myself to use the word. If I could have convinced anyone of the truth of such a claim, what would happen then? What would I have been party to? If you read this and judge me for it, then ask yourself what you would have done in my place.

The three of us booked in to the only hotel in

town. I could not look at the boy. An English actor - a famous one I was later told - and his manager, were checking in and the manager tried to coax the monster with cheerful words. If he had but known the truth!

As we parted in the corridor, Mrs Benson - though I strongly doubted that was her real name - whispered the word, 'Thank you' and those were the only words that passed between us. I could think of nothing to say and after a moment, I turned away and walked to my room, locking the door behind me.

I have never in my life been so desperate to see the busy streets of my home town, but I will wait another day. I hear the train whistle now and I hear the sound of footsteps in the hall. I know it's them. They have paused outside my door . . . and now they move on and away and I can breathe again.

I pray that our paths will never cross again.

There the journal entry ends and there my story ends also. There is nothing more to say. I can present no evidence as to the veracity of the account. I can only say that I see no reason for the lie and I do not detect the hand of a dreamer or a drunk.

Before I was released from my employment I had read a great many letters and journal entries by Henry F___ and I took him to be a very down to earth sort of man - a good man, a man I should have liked to meet; a far better man than his son, of that I am certain.

I will only add that it became a lifelong

obsession of mine to try and find some trace of that woman and her son in the historical record. Every archive I was given access to, I searched for any sign, any hint, of 'Mrs Benson' and her child, but so far as I have been able to discover, this journal entry was the only record of their existence.

***Chris Priestley** has found great success with his macabre stories for young readers. He is the author of the chilling and brilliant* Tales of Terror *series, the haunting* The Dead of Winter, *the fantastically frightening* Mister Creecher, *and the psychological thriller* Through Dead Eyes. *He is also a talented artist and illustrator. His cartoons have been published in* The Independent *and other national newspapers. Chris lives in Cambridge, where he continues to write his seriously scary stories. His website is www.chrispriestleybooks.com.*

THE CATCHER
Berni Stevens

London, 1849

A sudden flurry of snowflakes blurred my vision and the thin soles of my worn boots slipped momentarily on the icy cobbles. Pulling my threadbare coat tighter around my body, I gritted my teeth against the biting cold. I began to walk faster, feeling a sudden desperate need to reach the place I called home.

I knew the man followed me, even though he made no sound. There was no need to turn around again to see his tall thin form; a dark outline against a blanket of white.

It was the third night in a row the stranger had followed me home from my pitch near the theatre. To earn pennies I sold matches to the richly-dressed gentlemen on their way to the theatre with their mistresses. Then they can light their fat cigars whilst they watch the bawdy show. Gentlemen – they were not exactly *gentlemen* – how I hated their whisky-soaked breath and their roving eyes. I hated the fact that I had to bob a curtsey and call them 'Sir,' and I hated the fear that ran through my body like a knife, when their eyes lingered for too long on my breasts where they strained against the ill-fitting coat. *What did the man who followed me really want?*

I am sixteen years old, although sometimes I feel sixty. Home is an attic room in a three-storey house with my brother Tom – he's nineteen. Our parents died of the cholera when I was nine, and Tom has looked out for us both ever since. The house is cold and draughty, most of the windows were broken years ago, and the other folk who live in the house have nailed up bits of sacking to try and keep out the cold, the rain and the snow. It doesn't work. We're lucky in a way, Tom and me, living at the top of the house we're less likely to be robbed. Not that we have anything worth pinching. But I do have a book. It was my Mum's and I can't read it, but it's still my favourite thing.

At last I turned into our street, and had to hurriedly jump sideways when a bowl of slops was emptied into the street from a top window. All the houses look the same in our street; tall and thin and filled to the attics with people, drying laundry and crying babes. I could hear sounds of squabbling, the shrill nagging of the women above cussing from the men. It was always the same. Home sweet home. Most of the windows had candlelight spluttering behind the sack coverings: there's no gaslight in these houses.

At least the snow covered the rotting rubbish in the gutters and kept the rats away. Better than the summer, when the stench could make me retch and the rats grew bolder by the day. I preferred winter, even as I blew on my frozen, blue fingers and thought I'd never be warm again.

I risked a glance behind me as I pushed open our front door. The man stood in the road just as if he'd been frozen in time. I couldn't see his face, so I couldn't tell whether he was young or old. He stood up straight like a young man, yet seemed almost ageless. He was dressed all in black with a top hat on his head, and an opera cloak draped around his shoulders, like the ones the fancy gents wore to the theatre. He made no move to come any closer, just like the other nights, and still he didn't utter a sound.

'Clear off!' I shouted. He didn't move or speak. With a shudder, I went into the house, and slammed the door behind me. It didn't feel any warmer inside than out, that's for sure.

The people with a bit more money live in the parlours on the ground floor. Cobblers and fishmongers and the like. Our house always smells of fish and leather – amongst other things. Some of the people can afford bits of coal and they light fires in the iron grates, yet the house is still cold.

The attic felt a long way up as I made my way wearily up the creaking stairs. Tom sat at the small table in the corner, making matches. He looked up as I went in the room and nodded a greeting. He looked even thinner today, his skin a sallow colour against his coal black hair. The only brightness in his face was the bright blue of his eyes. He would have been good looking, my brother, if we'd had a bit more money and he'd got food in his belly.

'How did you fare, Ruby?' he asked, throwing his newest match into a basket.

I pulled the cloth purse from my pocket and

handed it to him. He opened it, and tipped the contents onto the table. Several pennies rolled out and clinked together as they landed. Tom nodded in satisfaction.

'Good girl.'

'I was followed again.' I tried to warm my frozen fingers over the flickering candle on the table.

'Same bloke?'

I nodded and Tom frowned. 'I should walk you back tomorrow.'

'The gents won't buy my matches if you're there.'

'Lechers, the lot of 'em.' Tom spat on the floor and gave me a guilty look when I made a disapproving noise.

'Is there anything to eat?' I changed the subject. I'm good at that.

Tom stood and crossed the room to a small cupboard over the stained sink. Opening the door, he pulled out a greasy-looking package and handed it to me.

'Bit of pie,' he said. 'You worked hard Ruby, you deserve it.'

'Have you had some?' I began stuffing pie into my mouth. It tasted stale and the pastry was soggy, but I was too hungry to care.

'I've eaten,' he sat back down and angled his chair onto its back legs in order to stare up at me. 'Need to get that wet coat off, before you catch your death.'

I finished the pie and began peeling off my wet coat. Tom pulled the moth-eaten blanket from the bed and handed it to me. I draped my coat over the back of the other chair and wrapped myself up in the thin blanket.

Tom set his chair back down and held his hands out. 'Give us your hands girl, and let me warm them for you.'

I sat in the other chair and placed my hands in his. 'Your hands are as cold as mine,' I smiled at him when he made an effort to rub my hands warm. I watched him concentrate on my hands, his dark hair flopping over his face. I often wondered what would happen if Tom met a girl he liked. I wondered whether he'd move her in here. Where would I go then?

'Tom . . . ?'

He looked up then and his eyes glinted in the candlelight.

'What if you want to get married?'

He snorted with amusement. 'Married? That's for people with money, girl – not for the likes of us.'

'What if you fall in love and want her to move in here?'

'More likely be you that takes the fancy of some bloke, don'cha think?' He grinned and letting go of my hands, he tugged at a long strand of my hair. 'Pretty little blonde, bound to attract someone soon.'

'Attract the wrong sort you mean.'

His smile faded and I realised he was remembering the rich old lechers near the theatre.

'Get yourself to bed, Rube, I'm going to get a tankard of ale at The Boar's Head before I turn in.'

'You're going out in this?'

'Don't fret, I won't be long.'

What is it with men and beer? I suspected Tom hadn't eaten a morsel but had saved his own coins to buy beer instead. I sighed as he pinched my cheek on his way out.

The door closed behind him and I went to the tiny window, pulling back the sacking so I could watch him walk up the street. After a few minutes, I saw the tall figure of my brother leave the house, and a cold hand of terror squeezed my heart when I saw the stranger in the top hat follow him.

I never heard Tom come back that night. I tried so hard to stay awake, and thought the cold would help, but must have fallen asleep sometime after the bells of Bow chimed three. He was there when I opened my eyes at six; his long lean frame huddled in the blanket on the edge of the narrow bed. He looked as still as death, and I'd seen a lot of that round here. I concentrated on the top part of his body and stared until I thought I saw a slight rise and fall. Not dead then. Not yet.

'Tom?'

No answer.

Something made me go to the window and move the sacking aside to look out. It was still dark but the snow made everything look brighter. The tall thin man stood exactly where I had last seen him, except this time he stared up at our window – at me. Stifling a scream, I let the sacking fall back; my heart pounding so hard I feared it would burst from my chest.

'Look again, Ruby, look again and he'll be gone . . .' I whispered a mantra to myself. With trembling hands I pushed the sacking back a tiny fraction. The man had gone. Tears trickled slowly down my cheeks, and I sat on the end of the bed, staring into space. *Who was he? What did he want?* Obviously he had wanted something to do with Tom, and now – apparently – with me too.

A slight noise from the bed made me look at my brother. His face had taken on a ghostly pallor and I feared he had a sickness. I moved to sit closer to him and put my hand on his brow. He felt like ice. His throat lay exposed and I went to pull the old blanket over him, when I noticed the marks. Two slightly rounded but jagged marks, evenly spaced, with dried blood crusted around the edges. Something had attacked him . . . but what?

'Tom?' I tried to rouse him but he didn't hear me. His chest barely rose now and I feared he would die if left alone. I rose to get my coat from the back of the chair and shrugged into it. Still damp from last night, the coat offered little warmth, and my fingers, numb with cold, wrestled with the fastenings.

'Please don't die, Tom,' I whispered. 'Don't leave me.'

How long I sat beside him I don't know, but I knew the day had almost gone because the shadows lengthened, and it became difficult to make out Tom's features in the gathering gloom. Still he didn't wake from his deathly slumber.

A sudden loud rap at the door startled me, and I jumped to my feet. Wrapping my arms around my body, I held my breath and kept perfectly still.

'Ruby,' a deep male voice said softly. 'Open

the door, child.'

He knew my name. *How did he know my name?* Somehow I knew the voice belonged to the man from outside. I stayed silent.

'Your brother is lost to you; only I can help you now.' The voice sounded almost reasonable. 'Open the door.'

I looked back at Tom. He didn't appear to be breathing at all now. As I watched, he suddenly sat up and turned to face me. My breath caught in my throat when I saw his eyes. They shone like a rat's eyes in candlelight. Hungry and malicious.

'Tom?' My voice was barely a whisper.

His smile was a parody of his usual smile. Lips stretched back from pale gums and sharp teeth. He didn't look like my brother any more.

'Ruby.' The voice outside sounded desperate.

I backed away from Tom without taking my eyes from his, and fumbled with the door handle behind me. I wrenched the door open at the same time Tom sprang across the room with the speed of a feral cat.

'Invite me in!' ordered the voice behind me.

Tom grasped me by the throat as I tried to call out, but his strong fingers dug into my windpipe and cut off my supply of air.

'Hallo little sister,' said Tom in a voice completely unlike the brother I loved. I struggled, gasping for air, my arms flailing – and he laughed. Black spots danced in front of my eyes and my breathing became laboured, and then the darkness overcame me.

When I opened my eyes again, the world was different. Tom sat on a chair, his arms and legs bound in silver chains. Blood-flecked spittle sprayed from his mouth when he snarled at the tall man who stood between us.

'Get up, Ruby,' the man said.

Obediently, I stood. A raging hunger swept through my body. Hunger and I were not exactly strangers, but this was different. My eyes went to the stranger . . . somehow I felt everything must be his fault.

'I am sorry, child,' he said.

'What happened?'

'You must both come with me now.'

I stared at him. Then he produced a length of silver chain and I understood.

Berni Stevens *lives in a 400-year-old cottage in Hertfordshire, with her husband, son and black cat. She trained in graphic design and has designed book covers for more than twenty years. Books and art remain her passion, and her love of the paranormal began when she read Bram Stoker's* Dracula. *She serves on the Committee of the Dracula Society. Berni has had several short stories published, and her first novel,* Fledgling, *was published in the US by The Wild Rose Press in 2011. The first book in her paranormal romance trilogy will be published in the UK in April 2014. She can be found at www.bernistevensdesign.com and www.bernistevens.blogspot.co.uk.*

SO MUCH THICKER THAN WATER
Sue Gedge

I step back and look with pride at the table I have prepared. Everything has been arranged in accordance with the ancient decrees of the Elders handed down to us from the days when our people still ruled the Land beyond the Forest. The starched white linen tablecloth, edged with lace, presented to Great-Grandmother Floresca in the Old Country when she was a veiled, virgin bride, lies smoothly on the heavy oak table.

Here are the pewter chalices, polished with the milk of goats, and there, arranged in neat circles on black plates, are the sesame biscuits that I baked before cockcrow under a crescent moon. The blood-red candles are set in circlets of ivy twined with hemlock. The heavy brocade curtains are drawn across the wide bay window, keeping out the unforgiving rays of the setting sun. I have done my best. Surely no one will find fault with me tonight?

The door swings open and the family enter.

First, Grandfather Radu, on the arm of his favourite daughter-in-law, Daciana, the proud, haughty beauty, widow of Brodgnar, he who perished in battle against the forces of the enemy. Daciana's midnight-blue silk dress drips with sequins and jewels; the family heirlooms, the gold chains and the string of black pearls are displayed across her ample chest, trophies of her matriarchal triumph. Her three tall, adult sons, Cosmo, Dragomir and Vladnar follow her, and next, heavy with child, a pumpkin about to burst, comes Dragomir's wife Alina. I have no sons, I have no imminent grandchild, and soon, no doubt, Daciana will find some subtle way of reminding me of this fact.

Petromir, my husband and master for twenty years, brings up the rear. The legs of the kill dangle over the sides of the platter as he holds it aloft. He lowers it onto the mahogany sideboard, as the family take their places, Grandfather Radu at the head of the table. I light the candles with all the solemnity befitting my role as hostess. Petromir slits the kill open from throat to rump. The chalices are filled with red, foaming liquid, the plates loaded with flesh. We, the Undying Ones, the descendants of the People beyond the Forest, are ready to feast.

First we bow our heads. Grandfather Radu utters the blessing in the old tongue and then, in perfect unison, we repeat the words in the language of our adopted country: *Remember the Home-Land, remember the rituals of blood. We are bound by blood, by the blood we share and by the blood we drink, the blood that gives us life and sets us apart. Let us give thanks for the blood.*

Keep the faith of the blood.

Now there is laughter as the feasting begins.

'A superb vintage!' Grandfather Radu takes a sip from his chalice. 'You keep a good cellar, Petromir. I congratulate you.'

'We can get better in Cricklewood,' I hear Daciana mutter under her breath. She looks across the table at me. 'And from where did you acquire the candles, my dear?' She asks softly.

'From the usual place,' I say. 'They are genuine beeswax, made by the bees that gather pollen from the lilac of the Old Country, from the *Syringa Josikaea,* and they have been dyed with the plasma of wolves.'

'Are you sure?' Daciana frowns. 'There are so many imitations in the market these days, made from the coarsest tallow. And it seems to me that the odour emanating from *those* isn't quite . . .'

'Can I cut you some rye bread, sister-in-law?' I seize the bone-handled bread knife and smile as I curse her in my heart.

'Did I ever tell you,' clutching his fork like a dagger, Grandfather Radu spikes up a gobbet of rare, moist flesh, 'The story my grandfather told me? Long before the Great War, he was chopping wood for his father on a snowy evening when he met the Count himself. His Eminence was travelling across the Borgo Pass in a carriage drawn by four, snorting black stallions, and their icy breath filled the air. My grandfather was only a lad, but the Count raised his hat to him and said . . .' His voice trails off. It seems that, once again, he has forgotten exactly what it was the Count was reputed to have said.

'Grandpa,' Vladnar smiles at him indulgently. 'Do you know that there isn't a single bi-centenarian amongst the People who doesn't make exactly the same claim as you? But, since you have mentioned him, I propose a toast. The Count!' He raises his chalice. The soft, flickering light of the burning candles glints upon pewter.

'The Count!' With an exuberant cry, the family follow suit.

For a moment, I almost feel a part of the joy in the room, but a moment later, my spirits sink. Just as the toast was being proposed, she slunk into the room. Now she's scowling, slumped in her seat, thumping the toe of her black velvet slipper against the leg of the table, a picture of teenage rebellion. Becca, my daughter.

I know what will happen now. She won't touch her meat; she won't drink from her chalice. I glance at her; I raise an eyebrow. She shrugs, then dips her little finger into the red liquid. A moment later, she wipes it on the underside of the tablecloth. It will take her until the next Gathering to finish her drink at this rate. And there's something else. She's wearing a t-shirt under her black robe, and I can just read the printed words: *So long, Suckers.* Oh, the disgrace! Where can she have acquired such an abomination? Certainly not from the trunk containing the remnants of Great-Grandmother Floresca's trousseau, I can be sure of that.

Petromir has noticed her behaviour. The look he gives her is as sharp and swift as a sabre flash. Apparently obedient, she lifts her chalice to her mouth and takes a sip, but a moment later, she pushes back her chair and hurtles from the room. I rise, bow with due deference to Grandfather Radu, avoid the eyes of Daciana and follow her. I find Becca bending over the basin in the downstairs cloakroom, gagging audibly, her elbows sticking out from her sides like the wings of an emaciated, plucked chicken.

'Not even human blood tonight and still you do not feast!' The words burst out before I can stop myself.

'It makes me puke, Mum,' Becca turns to me, wiping her mouth on her sleeve. 'I can't drink that stuff. It's *weird*. I'm not drinking no more blood.'

'You must not speak like that!' I gasp. 'Where is your grammar?'

'And I'm not eating that muck neither,' she adds.

'It was you, wasn't it?' The realisation hits me as hard as a stake to the chest. '*You* were the one who buried that flesh in the soil around the mandragora plant last week.'

'Yeah, Mum, it was,' she admits. 'I like my meat cooked.'

'What do you mean by spurning our food?' I retort. 'Don't you know how important it is to follow the traditions of the Elders? All through history, the People have been persecuted, driven from the Home-Lands, forced to hide themselves from the light. The day that the People cease to celebrate the Blood Feast will be the day that we die. We must never forget the Land beyond the Forest. We must honour the Count. We must . . .'

'I've heard it Mum.' Becca shrugs. 'I've heard it a million times. And it's creepy, disgusting crap!'

'Such blasphemy!'

'I didn't ask to be part of this family,' the girl is relentless. 'They're all mad. Cousin Vladnar is always groping my knee under the table. Grandfather Radu smells like a stable. And the feast is foul. At Chantelle's house they have burger and fries. And fish fingers. And they drink Coke and Dr Pepper.'

I feel as though the breath has been sucked out of me. My chest is tight with the pain. I can hardly bear the weight of my daughter's confession.

'*You have been mixing with the Out Siders*?' I stare at her.

'Yes, Mum. I have,' she is defiant and unashamed. 'I had tea at Paris's house last week. We had pizza.'

'You have *eaten* the food of the Out Siders?' My mouth feels so dry I can hardly speak.

'You have partaken of their drink?'

'Yeah,' she nods vigorously. 'It was cool.'

'Don't you see what you have done?' I feel sick to my stomach. 'As a result of your apostasy you have caught one of their diseases! I have read of this illness, a wasting complaint that afflicts the young Out Siders. They do not eat, they grow pale and thin, they hide food, they refuse to feast, or worse still, they gorge on impure comestibles, on chocolate and crisps, and then they go to the bathroom and they . . .'

What is it I see in Becca's eyes? Contempt? Or is it just pity?

'You can't *catch* anorexia or bulimia, Mum. It's not contagious. And there's nothing wrong with me. I'm OK, right? I just want to be normal.'

'But how did you meet these people?' I persist. 'This 'Chantelle', this 'Paris'? Such barbaric names!'

'I go to school with them.'

'*You have been out in the day time! In sunlight?*'

'Yeah!' Becca pops a gobbet of bubble gum into her mouth, chews and then blows. 'And guess what,' she sucks the pink scum back into her mouth. 'I never combusted.'

'Becca, that's impossible.' I put my hand out to steady myself, clutching the edge of the hand-basin, remembering how I pushed her pram through the streets at midnight, keeping my baby safe.

'No, it isn't, Mum, there aren't any vampires. It's all a myth.'

'Is that what they've taught you at *that school*?'

'Nah. They never mentioned it. But they let anybody in, even a loner like me. Only now, I don't feel such a loner any more. I've made friends. And I'm moving out. My bag's packed and I'm going to go and live at my boyfriend's.'

'But you're so young.' Now I'm pleading with her. 'It isn't safe out there.'

'Get real, Mum. It's far worse in here. You ought to leg it, too.'

'*Becca . . .*'

But she's slipped past me, into the hall. A moment later, I hear the front door open, then bang shut. I splash water on to my face and turn to the doorway. My stomach lurches; Petromir is standing there, his eyes flaming with accusation.

'What is this?' he seizes my wrist. 'How

dare you leave the Feast? Such an insult to the family! Would you be a traitor to the ties of blood?'

'Petromir, it's Becca. She . . .'

Petromir tightens his grasp on my wrist. He has strong hands, dangerous hands. I've seen him strangle foxes on Clapham Common.

'Let the girl go,' he hisses. 'She is but trash.'

The whole family must have heard Becca's departure, but no one remarks upon it as I return to the table. Petromir, too, resumes his seat. I know that later, when we are alone, he will give vent to his anger. The candlelight plays on his fine, high cheekbones and I flinch, seeing the way he bares his sharp, white teeth and bites on his sesame biscuit.

I was only a girl when my parents brought me to this country and arranged our wedding, only a little older than Becca. I remember how Grandfather Radu tied the red ribbons around my wrists and neck to symbolise the bloodline that was to be strengthened by my union with Petromir. *Do you promise never to stray, to remain pure?* And I said nothing of my secret, my fear that I might not be one of them at all. I said nothing of my mother's deathbed confession, that my parents had adopted me as a baby, or rather, my father had stolen me from a crib in the maternity hospital in Prague where he worked as a night porter. And now, purely for business reasons, I was to be allied with the family Radu and . . . how could I have allowed it to happen?

All these long years, trying to keep their customs and never quite succeeding. Twenty years married to Petromir, a handsome man but without a shred of tenderness in his soul, if indeed he has a soul. Can I really regret that day, fourteen years ago, when, in broad daylight, I opened the door and let in . . . ? No! I must not think of that, not here, not now. Reputedly, there are mind-readers in Petromir's family and Daciana is staring at me. I must think of something else, I must think of . . .

I try to focus on the conversations that are taking place up and down the table.

Alina, her almond eyes wide with pregnant rapture, is describing the antique carved wooden cradle that has been passed down in her family since time immemorial. Grandfather Radu is rambling on about the Old Country. Petromir is silent. Cosmo and Dragomir are boasting about their last hunting expedition, lamping for deer in Richmond Park, in their SUV with the blacked-out windows, and how once they chased a group of young Out Siders, hurling their spears and yelling medieval war cries. They have broken the law of our adopted country over and over again, and as for the family business, Night-Cabs, it was only intended that fares should be taken from those of our kind as they hurried home to beat the dawn. And then came the night when Brodgnar saw that girl just by the cemetery, pulled to the kerb and . . .

'How dare you think of that!' Daciana spits the words across the table at me.

'I said nothing,' I gaze at her, affecting innocence. 'But since you mention it, your husband was justly punished.'

'We are not bound by the laws of the Out Siders!'

'No,' I agree, sweetly. 'But nevertheless, a sunlit police cell in Finchley did prove somewhat inconvenient, did it not? What do you think of my sesame biscuits, by the way? Can I offer you another?'

'Bitch!' Daciana stabs a black olive with her fork. 'Who are you to point the finger of blame? Do you think I don't know? Who was he? Becca's father? Not one of us, I'll be bound.'

'They have a saying in this country,' It seems that Grandfather Radu, deep in his own ramblings, hasn't heard a word of my barbed exchange with my sister-in-law. '*Blood is thicker than water*. And so it is. When I look around this table, and think of our ties of blood, the consanguinity of family . . .'

'Are you sure that's what it means?' I suggest. 'Might it not mean that blood is inferior when it comes to imbibing? That it's such a glutinous, bitter, cloying gunge, so less desirable than the clear, refreshing liquid that runs from the tap?'

'Be silent!' Petromir slaps the flat of his hand on the table. The pewter chalices jump. 'No one cares for your opinions.'

'Perhaps not,' I rise from my chair. 'But if the phrase does allude to family, then there is only one person to whom I feel such a connection. Becca, my uncouth, self-willed but brave daughter, who is as we speak, making her own way in the world and whom I intend to follow. This may come as a shock to you all, but the truth is . . .'

'The man who came to read the electricity meter.' Daciana's voice rings out like the bell before an execution. 'So that's who it was. Did you really think you'd get away with it? Didn't you realise there would be consequences?'

They're all staring at me now, their eyes flashing anger and vengeance. Petromir, Daciana, Grandfather Radu, Cosmo, Dragomir, Vladnar and Alina. Does everyone hate their in-laws, as much as I hate mine, I wonder? He was nice, that man who came to read the meter. His name was Stan, and he had a tattoo of a rose on his left buttock. Yes, Daciana, he did! Ha!

'Consequences, yes,' I walk over to the window. 'But for whom, I wonder?'

'What are you doing?' Daciana's voice has sunk to a whimper. She's actually afraid. Now there's a result.

'Rather too dark in here, don't you think?' I grasp the gold curtain cord. 'You said yourself that the candles were inferior.'

There's no going back now, I tell myself, as I prepare to tug the cord. After this, I'm leaving. But first, I need to find out what really does happen when you let in the light. It might not work, of course. The sun may have already gone down or it may all be a myth. Either way, I don't care what happens to this blood-sucking clan of control freaks. After all, they're not my flesh and blood.

Sue Gedge *has had articles and short stories in a number of publications, including* The Times Educational Supplement, The Oldie, All Hallows, Supernatural Tales, The Mechanics Institute Review *and* The Romantic Novelists' Association *anthology* Loves Me, Loves Me Not, *but she has yet to find a publisher for her vampire novel,* The Practical Woman's Guide to Living with the Undead. *Her passions include Victorian cemeteries,* Being Human, *bats, ravens, Mervyn Peake, the Brontes, Terence Stamp,* Withnail and I, *Richard III,* Les Miserables, *Professor Severus Snape, Spike from* Buffy, *ghost stories and drinking full-blooded red wine by moonlight.*

NOBODY GOES TO THE CASTLE

Katherine Haynes

Carrie swore as the first soft flakes drifted against the windscreen. Snow still lay deep in the mountains, but she had hoped no more would fall. It was early May and friends of hers had complained of the heat when visiting Romania the previous year.

Everything had gone wrong this morning, from her having overslept to the failure of her hire car to be ready on time. She had set out far later than planned.

The snow began to come down harder and harder. She switched on the windscreen wipers, alarmed at how quickly the fields on either side of the road were disappearing under the whiteness. At least it was warm inside the car, she had a flask of soup, an electric torch and her paraphernalia; she should be safe enough.

As the afternoon wore on, she saw less and less traffic on the road. Seemingly black flakes tumbled and swirled through the air, appearing white only when they landed. The windscreen wipers swished from side to side, making a soothing rhythm, but she had a long way to go yet and the car was crawling now.

Radu, Elena and Vasile were expecting her. She had never met them, but they had corresponded regularly; originally by letter and now, with the advance of technology, by e-mail. She had tried to call them or text a message, but her mobile phone didn't work in this mountainous region.

She glanced at the clock on the dashboard and saw that it was already ten-to-four. They had been expecting her to reach the castle by five o'clock. Well, she couldn't possibly make it by then, but at least they wouldn't be worried just yet.

The fields had given way to pine trees, while the road wound up and down and up once more. She drove even slower, frightened of skidding, of crashing through the trees. In her mind's eye she imagined the car breaking through the pines, rolling over and over, striking rocks, bouncing, falling until it lay upside down at the bottom of a gully, all its lights and windows smashed, herself smashed inside it. How long would she survive in the cold? She had heard there were bears in the woods. Bears and wolves. Tourists were encouraged to come here on hunting expeditions. Would she be lucky enough to be found by a hunter, or would a bear get to her first?

She was relieved when the road descended again, became level. Houses began to appear, some of them very similar to one another, like bungalows, others more individual, with a tower here, a zinc roof there, one house with an elaborately carved gate.

Carrie stopped for petrol.

'*Cât costă?*' she asked and handed over a handful of lei.

The garage attendant looked at her gloomily, took some notes and coins, then gave the rest of her money back.

'*Mulțumesc.*'

'*Cu plăcere.*'

It was lonely back on the road and she could barely see by this time. There was no way she was going to reach the castle before dark. No doubt the others would realise she had got caught in the snowstorm. She would ring them as soon as possible... How could she have been so stupid! She might have been able to use a phone at the petrol station! Carrie cursed herself for not thinking of it sooner. Oh, well, there was nothing she could do about it now.

Time passed and, as she had feared, night fell and she still hadn't reached her destination. She was driving in darkness, all but blinded by the snow. The journey began to feel like a nightmare which would never end.

All at once, she saw a light. *Thank God,* she thought.

There was another light and then another. She was driving through a village. The sensible thing to do would be to stop, to see if there was a hotel or a pub. It would be good to have something hot to drink - her soup was long gone - and something to eat. She could use the loo and the phone. If there was one.

Carrie parked the car next to a promising looking building and was glad, when she emerged into the snow, to see that it was a bar called the *Capra Neagră*.

Once inside, she began to explain in her halting Romanian that she was late for an appointment. Luckily the barman interrupted her and she was relieved to learn he spoke English.

There was no telephone, but she used the lavatory and ordered a meal. The barman recommended 'the trout fish and chipped potatoes.' He provided the usual welcoming glass of tuica, with the customary offering of bread and salt, then showed her to a table.

There were stuffed animals - real ones, not toys - displayed on the beams holding up the ceiling and Carrie, sipping her plum brandy, found this in poor taste, though she supposed that they were there to encourage the hunting. The whole bar had a very masculine quality. There hadn't even been a mirror in the Ladies and all the other customers were male.

The barman, who told her his name was Georges, brought over her meal himself. She washed the fish down with Bergenbier. Following this she ate a pancake with jam, a popular local dish.

'It is the coldestest night this month,' explained Georges when she had finished eating.

Smiling a little, knowing in her heart of hearts that it was both rude and wrong to criticise his quaint English, she replied,

'Yes, it is very cold and the snow's terrible. I was due at Castel Nimeni at five, but . . .'

'Nobody goes to the castle,' said Georges.

'Nobody,' put in another man.

Carrie thought of the letters she had received,

the messages. Radu had told her he was the owner of the castle, but she didn't really know anything about him.

'Why not?' she asked.

'Is ruin. Was burned down, then rebuildeded, then burned again.'

'I thought it was inhabited. I've been in correspondence with someone who lives there.'

Georges shrugged.

'Maybe is joke. Castle is ruin.'

Radu had said he owned the castle, but he had never actually claimed to live there. Perhaps he had asked Carrie to meet him there because it was an easy landmark for her to find and had intended that they would drive on to his house. Why, he might even live in this very village. Carrie asked if Georges knew him, but the barman shook his head.

At that moment there was a howl from outside, a long, lonely, eerie sound which made Carrie's hair stand on end. Goose pimples swept her flesh as if a bucket of icy water had been poured over her.

'What the hell was that?'

'Is wolf,' said Georges simply.

Carrie looked again at the stuffed red squirrel above her head. This was forest country, hunting country, the home of wolves and bears and wild boar. It was cold and dark outside, more snow was falling. Only a fool would venture forth on a night like this; no way was she going to try and find some old ruin.

'Have you got any rooms?' she asked.

'Rooms?'

'Somewhere I could stay, sleep?'

'*Da.*'

'Thank you,' she said.

'Is no problem.'

Georges sent a boy to help her with her things. She fetched her luggage from the car, which was now almost buried in the snow. It probably wouldn't have started, even if she had wanted to proceed with her journey.

The bedroom was fitted out with very basic furniture, but there was a bathroom just along the corridor from it and at least she was out of the storm. Drowsy with tiredness and the effects of the alcohol she'd consumed, she tried her mobile again, but without success, then wrote up her diary for the day. Proud of her poor Romanian, she scrawled, '*Am o camera.*'

A tinkling sound, like the gentle jingle of wind chimes, woke Carrie in the dead of night. She lay rigid in the bed. '*Dorm in pat,*' - 'I sleep in the bed,' - echoed over and over in her mind, as she strained her ears to listen. What was it? The sound became louder and she realised that it was laughter; hard, cruel laughter.

It was freezing and she became aware that the window was open, the snow drifting in. She could see clearly because the moon had risen and was shining into the room. The snowflakes danced and whirled in the moonlight, began to gather together, to take shape, to fashion themselves into the images of people. The shadowy forms of three young women stood before her. She could see the brightness of their eyes and mouths.

'No!' breathed Carrie.

She wanted to leap from the bed, to reach for her bag, but she felt petrified, unable to move.

The door of the room swung open and she could see Georges standing there. He smiled, showing his teeth.

'I invite them in,' he said and Carrie shrieked as the women approached, bending towards her, licking their lips.

All night Radu had paced back and forth, to and fro, looking at his watch, jumping at any sound which might indicate a passing car. Elena had watched him, a frown on her pretty face. She had gone to the tower window every so often, gazed out at the snow, tried to assure him that there was no point in expecting Carrie tonight. Only Vasile had gone to bed and to sleep.

Morning came and there was no sign of their expected guest, no message. As time passed and there was still no news, Radu grew more and more agitated. Elena tried to get him to eat some breakfast, but he couldn't summon up any appetite.

'My God,' he said suddenly, turning to his companions, 'you don't think she went to the village, do you?'

'Surely she wouldn't have gone there alone, without us?'

'She might not have realised where she was. She could have got lost.'

'We had better go and see,' said Elena.

The snow had stopped and the sun was shining. Vasile drove. It took them forty minutes to reach the village. From the state of the buildings and the condition of the roads, it was clear that the place had been deserted for some time. The few vehicles on the verges were rusty, some of them with flat tyres and broken windscreens. Only one car stood out; the one parked outside the Capra Neagră.

Radu pushed the door of the bar. It creaked on its hinges and opened onto a foul-smelling room, full of dust and debris. A single set of footprints in the dust showed Carrie's progress from the door to the counter to the table. They followed the prints to the foot of the stairs. Radu led the way up.

'Careful!' he cried to his companions, as one of the treads bent under his weight.

They coughed in the rank atmosphere and moved up the stairs with caution, keeping close to the wall.

Vasile opened one door, which proved to be that of a bathroom. As he had expected, there were no mirrors on the walls. The next door he tried swung open easily, its movement all but propelling them into the room. Elena couldn't help letting out a cry, as she saw what lay upon the bed.

Vasile put his arms around her and drew her away, while Radu - suddenly overcome by grief - made his way across the uneven floor.

He had hoped for so much from Carrie. She was well known in her field and he couldn't understand how someone like her, a supposed 'expert,' could have fallen victim like this to those she hunted.

His letters and e-mail messages had brought her here, all the way from England to Bucharest, then on to 'the land beyond the forest,' and now she sprawled here, drained and dead. The marks of fangs were on her neck and wrists and one of her own three-foot stakes had been hammered through her heart.

Katherine Haynes *has been a member of the Dracula Society for thirty years, during which time she has served on Committee, edited Voices from the Vaults from* ***1989-1998****, been a member of the literary committee and helped to arrange various meetings and events. For her, the Society is a kind of extended family and in its company she has enjoyed the opportunity to meet interesting people, do unusual things and visit far-flung places. Tours of Romania were clearly the inspiration behind her story. Katherine lives in Hertfordshire with artist and model-maker Vince Mattocks. Visitors to their home have been known to comment, 'You like vampires, then?'*

THE COFFIN
Anna Taborska

Jack lived a stone's throw from the rear gate of the cemetery, so it made perfect sense for him to cut through the vast necropolis to get to the tube. Jack wasn't particularly fond of cemeteries – not like those people who took photos of derelict graveyards or paid good money to visit burial grounds with famous residents. He'd certainly never planned to live near one, but when his childless aunt died and left him her house, he wasn't going to look the proverbial gift horse in the mouth. And the walk through the cemetery wasn't altogether unpleasant. So the fifteen minutes cut from Jack's commute to work – and another fifteen minutes from his trek back again – made it worth having to walk past all those dead people, and occasional living ones too.

The worst was when there was a funeral on. Jack hated that. It made him feel like an interloper – intruding on people's private grief. So whenever he saw a priest and a group of mourners at a freshly dug grave, he would slope past and out of the cemetery even quicker than usual.

Today was no exception. As Jack hurried along the central avenue to the main gate at the far end, he saw a coffin some way away from the path he was traversing. A furtive glance told him that, although the coffin was positioned next to a freshly dug grave, there were no mourners or gravediggers nearby. Strange for a coffin to be left unattended like that. Perhaps the mourners had left and the gravediggers hadn't arrived yet.

Jack hastened through the cemetery, out the main gate and across the road to the underground station. From there the tube ferried him – with two changes along the way - to the offices of Lidell and Lidell, where he worked as an administrator.

Jack forgot all about the coffin – until, that is, he was on his way home and striding through the cemetery once more. This time he could afford a more leisurely pace. The sun was beginning to set, but the cemetery wouldn't close for at least another hour. Jack relished the last of the day's sun; the air had a pleasant temperature to it despite the days already getting shorter. Then something caught his eye: something glinting in the setting sun. It stood on the end of the grass verge, almost spilling out onto the central avenue. Whatever it was, it stood between Jack and the rear gate, and, unless he took a detour, which would involve weaving in and out of the tombstones and crosses, he would have to walk right past it.

Jack slowed down and squinted myopically in the direction of the large, pallid object. As he got closer, he wondered why it had taken him so long to recognise the elongated hexagonal form. It was a coffin, carved in a pale wood, which just now glowed as it caught the sun's last rays. Then it was plunged into a dim half-light, as dusk fell quickly.

A coffin in a cemetery – not really a combination to be wondered at, and yet something about the casket made Jack nervous. Not only was it placed far too close to the path – almost pushing out onto it – but, Jack finally realised, it was the same coffin he'd seen earlier in the day. Still unattended, but in a different position than when he'd been rushing to work. Weird. But not weird enough to make him turn back and take the long way home. Jack decided not to take a detour along a different path through the cemetery either, but scurried on, as far from the casket as the wide central avenue would allow, eyes fixed firmly on the path ahead.

As he scuttled past the coffin and on towards the exit gate, Jack became aware of his own heartbeat. Once he estimated that he was past the offending container, he released the breath he hadn't realised he'd been holding. After twenty more metres or so, Jack slowed down. He planned to reach the exit gate without looking back, but then decided that he was being stupid. Aiming to put his mind at ease, he paused and turned around, nearly jumping out of his skin at what he saw. The coffin was no longer at the edge of the central avenue: it was right in the middle of it, and only ten metres or so from where Jack was standing. It was a trick of the light, he thought; a case of false perspective. There was no one around to move the coffin and therefore the coffin could not have moved.

But as Jack set off rapidly for the exit once more, he cast another glance behind him. And this time there was no mistaking it. The distance between him and the pale-coloured casket had shrunk by at least a couple of metres.

Jack ran for the gate, his heart pounding fiercely in his chest. He never saw the coffin move, but each time he glanced over his shoulder, the horrid object had gained a little more ground. Finally Jack was nearing the exit gate, but as it came into full view his prayers that the caretaker hadn't locked it early dwindled to a hoarse whimper; the gate was shut.

'Oh God!' Jack threw himself at the gate and rattled it vigorously. It swung open. 'Thank you!' Not locked; just closed – probably by some overzealous visitor on his or her way out. Without looking back, Jack slammed the gate shut behind him and darted for the safety of his front door, all the while telling himself that he hadn't just heard the scrape of wood on paving stone.

A couple of large vodkas and several cautious glances out of the window later, Jack managed to convince himself that he'd imagined the entire coffin episode. After all, with the audit and everything else that was going on at work, he hadn't been sleeping at all well lately. And everyone knows that the mind plays tricks – especially on the sleep-deprived and in that strange half-light between day and dusk.

Perhaps the shortcut through the graveyard was not such a good idea after all. Maybe he should bite the bullet and start going the long way around. Particularly now that darkness was falling earlier. Besides, the extra walk would do him good. The paunch he was starting to grow didn't hang well on his otherwise skinny frame.

After a microwave dinner and a couple of hours' television, Jack drank a final shot of vodka and called it a day. The alcohol knocked him out for an hour or two, but then he woke with a start. Afraid for no apparent reason, he reached out for the bedside light, but a sudden noise at the far side of his room startled him and he jerked his arm in alarm, knocking the flimsy lamp off the small cabinet.

'Shit!'

The crash as the lamp hit the floor told Jack that the bulb had probably smashed, but in any case, he had no time to find out as the shuffling, scraping sound came again, this time closer than before.

'Oh God!' Jack froze, and just then the waxing moon emerged from behind a cloud, casting enough light into the bedroom to propel Jack's fear to a new level.

Incomprehension and terror fought for control of Jack's mind as he tried to apprehend what he was seeing. It was standing at the foot of his bed, glimmering a pale silvery blue in the moonlight. The bedroom door and window were closed. In any case, the damned thing would not have fit through the window, and there was no sign of broken glass.

Jack had to get out of the bedroom. Out of the house. Without taking his eyes off the casket, he tried to pull off his duvet and swing his legs out of bed, but found himself no longer master of his own body.

As he finally succeeded merely in clenching his fists into tight, painful balls, the coffin at the foot of his bed started to groan and creak in a most alarming way. The pallid wood splintered and, as Jack watched, speechless, a clawed hand thrust its way heavenward from the hideous box, followed by another, and then the planks of the coffin were being pushed apart with inhuman strength, splinters raining down and nails popping out like champagne corks on New Year's Eve.

Jack couldn't move and he couldn't look away from the abomination that pulled itself nimbly out of the shattered wood and hissed at him through large yellow teeth that tapered to razor-sharp points. Its bloodshot eyes bored into Jack's, rooting him to the spot like an animal caught in the headlights of an approaching juggernaut. The cold metal slats of the headboard pressed into Jack's back as he pushed himself as far away as he could from the fetid, hairless monstrosity that now lurched towards him.

And as the fiend's foul stench enveloped him, Jack finally managed to close his eyes, the scream cut short in his throat as the creature's fangs sank in.

Jack hadn't missed a day's work in nine years, so when he didn't show up at the office for three days or answer any phone calls, his concerned boss contacted the police.

The officers had never seen such a hideous expression of terror on anyone's face. There was an infected wound on the victim's neck, and the body had been drained of blood. Even before the police pathologist was called in, Inspector Dougall knew that the case would never be solved. There were no signs of forced entry, and nothing appeared to be out of place. Only a large pile of pale, splintered, rotting wood at the foot of the hapless man's bed.

***Anna Taborska** is a filmmaker and horror writer. She has written and directed two short fiction films, two documentaries and the award-winning TV drama* The Rain Has Stopped. *Her stories have been published in a number of anthologies in the UK and the US, including* Best New Writing 2011, Best New Werewolf Tales Volume 1 *and* The Best Horror of the Year Volume 4. *Anna's debut short story collection,* For Those who Dream Monsters, *is due out in late 2013, with the release of a novelette collection,* Bloody Britain, *planned for 2014. Anna joined The Dracula Society in 2009.*

MISTER BITEY
Tony Lee

'Mister Bitey doesn't like you,' Kevin muttered almost to himself. 'Mister Bitey thinks that you should *die.*'

Richard looked down from the dining room table at his younger brother, currently playing with a small metal car on the carpet.

'What?' he asked.

Kevin looked up at Richard, smiling placidly.

'I said Mister Bitey doesn't like you,' he repeated. 'And that he thinks that you should die. He doesn't like most people. Apart from Mrs Jennings.'

Richard looked over to his mother, currently watching *Jeremy Kyle* on the television.

'Did you hear that?' he asked.

'Yes dear, your brother's imaginary friend doesn't like you,' his mother's eyes never left the television as she spoke. 'Don't worry; I'm sure you'll grow on him, just like you did on us.'

'But *Mum . . .*'

Richard's mother turned from the television to stare at her son with a steely eye.

'Richard, he's six. I somehow don't think that this is going to affect him that much. After all, Mister Bitey *is* imaginary.'

'Don't knock imaginary friends, Rose,' Richard's father now walked into the room, slumping onto the sofa beside his wife. 'Remember the one that Ricky had when he was Kevin's age?'

'I never had an imaginary friend!'

'Mister Growly, I think he was called. Something like a German Shepherd dog, in jeans and Converse trainers.'

Richard wanted to reply, to say that this was silly and childish, but as his mother spoke he started to remember something, something from a long time ago.

'They were red,' he said.

'That's the one,' his father smiled. 'He went everywhere with you for a year. And then one day, he was gone.'

Richard noted the look that his father then gave Kevin, still playing with his small metal car.

'And we hope that Kevin will do the same.'

'It's nothing,' Richard's mother rose irritably from the sofa. 'Just a phase.'

'I bloody hope so. You weren't the one that had to apologise to the headmaster for what he said to Mrs Jennings. I mean, where do you get that sort of language from at his age? To say your imaginary friend wants to marry your teacher is one thing, but to then say that he also wants to cut off her face and eat it, and suck on an eyeball until it -'

'Derek!' Richard's mother motioned towards Richard with her eyes. 'Enough.'

'Fine,' Richard's father rose from the sofa.

'I'm just saying it's creepy, that's all. We haven't seen that lad Ranjesh over here since he told him that 'Mister Bitey' wanted to use him as a *chew toy*, either.'

'Six year olds need an active imagination.'

'No Rose, *that* six year old needs *behavioural therapy.*'

And with that Richard's father left the room. Richard stared down at his younger brother, still playing with his car. As if sensing this, Kevin placed the toy down and looked up at him.

'Soon,' he said.

It was three days later when Richard heard the news about Mrs Jennings. She'd not been at school and eventually someone had gone to check on her, finding that the police had already beaten them to her house on Primrose Street. The teachers had told the assembly that she'd died peacefully in her sleep, but Billy Ryan in Year Seven said after school had ended that his dad was a paramedic and he'd heard that she was found in the bath, naked, and with her face torn off. All the other boys had laughed about the word *naked*, but it was the last part that terrified Richard. If it was true, how had Kevin known this would happen?

Richard had walked the streets after hearing the news, the winter sky darkening into night as he did so, and looking up he saw that he was now on Acacia Avenue, where the Patels lived. Walking up to the door and ringing the bell, he waited.

'Hello,' he said to the tall Indian woman

that faced him across the threshold. 'I'm Kevin Harker's brother. I was just wondering if Ranjesh was okay? We haven't seen him in a few days.'

'He's fine, just a little sickly.' The woman turned to close the door, but something in her eyes made Richard step forward, blocking the door from closing.

'What's up with him?' he asked.

The woman paled, pushing Richard away from the door as she slammed it in his face.

'Don't come back!' she shouted through the door.

Confused and now alone on the street, Richard stumbled backwards from the front door.

'Poor Ranjesh isn't having a good time of late,' the voice spoke behind him. 'He's lost a lot of blood somehow; he's pale and sickly, doesn't like bright light and won't eat his mother's curries when they have garlic in them.'

Richard spun around to find himself facing an old man, tanned skin, his brow lined with age, wild dark brown hair flecked with grey framing it. He was tall, and a shapeless grey tweed overcoat hid from view whether this man was skinny, fat or muscular. All that could be seen were the bottoms of a pair of blue jeans and a pair of battered red trainers.

'Hello,' the old man said.

'Um, I was told never to speak to strangers,'

'Yes, that's very proper,' the old man replied, nodding. 'But I'm not a stranger. I've known your family for many years.'

'I was especially told never to speak to strangers who claimed that they knew my family.'

'And what of your brother, eh? And the

vampire that has him enthralled?'

'I was also told that on no circumstances should I speak to strangers who claimed that they knew my family and believed in vampires,' Richard started to back away. 'And if you can excuse me, I think I need to -'

'Richard Harker,' the old man boomed. 'The time of games is now over. Search your memory. I knew you well. I was your defender. And now I must help your brother.'

Richard stared in shock at the old man, at his wild brown hair, his dark skin, his tweed overcoat, his tattered, mud splattered jeans and his dirty red trainers...

Converse trainers.

'Mister . . . Growly?' he whispered.

The old man smiled, his teeth sharp and glinting in the light of the streetlamp. Richard looked around the street, looking for some other witness of this confrontation.

'You're not real,' he said. 'You were just an imaginary friend!'

'Just like the one that speaks to your brother?' Mister Growly waggled his finger. 'There are more things in this world than what a boy can understand, you know.'

'Mister Bitey,' Richard said. 'What is he?'

'I've already said. He's a vampire,' Mister Growly replied. 'Although his name isn't 'Mister Bitey'. That's a name your brother's given him. His true name is Count Orlok Von Bloodsplatter, and he's a very nasty piece of work.'

'And he's in my brother's head? Is he invisible?'

'No, it is simply a mental connection,' the

old man rummaged around in his tweed coat, eventually pulling out a mouldy lump of cheese. With a smile he wolfed it down, licking his lips before continuing.

'It is easier to show, rather than tell,' he continued. 'Come; see with your own eyes.'

With that the old man turned and started off down the street, leaving Richard alone in the road, caught in a crossroads as to whether he should follow the old man to wherever, or return home to a brother that quite possibly talked to a vampire.

Eventually, he chose the former.

The night was well underway by the time that Mister Growly led Richard to Westenra Park. In the daylight this was a place of joy, with swings and roundabouts to play on, but at night the park was cold and lonely.

'I know this place,' Richard whispered. 'Mum brings Kevin here.'

'I know. How do you think Orlok gained his hold on your brother?' the old man replied, looking out across the park. 'But we're not here to discuss that. We're here to see this.'

Richard stared across the grass, following Mister Growly's outstretched finger at a couple of late teens, sitting on a bench. A boy and girl, they were kissing each other, unaware of the world around them.

'There,' Mister Growly hissed.

Richard felt a shiver of ice run down his back as he watched the shadows of the park start to move together, to coalesce into a tall, dark figure. Nothing more than a shape, the figure was cloaked and, as it watched the two teenagers kissing, Richard believed that it was *smiling*.

The young man pulled away from the girl as he noticed the approaching stranger, rising to his feet to confront the cloaked man. Richard couldn't hear what was being said, but it was obvious that the teenage boy was unhappy to find his evening interrupted. Richard watched as the young man stepped forward, suddenly stopping as the stranger rose a hand into the air, palm facing him. As if frozen in place the young man stood immobile as the cloaked stranger walked closer, moving around him, sniffing him as, with outstretched hand he froze the girl in place as well.

'This is your brother's imaginary friend,' Mister Growly said. 'Not so imaginary, is he?'

Richard shook his head as, across the park the stranger leaned over the young man, his mouth moving towards the throat. And then, with a sharp, snapping motion he sunk his teeth into the young man's neck, the dark blood spraying up as the artery was punctured, the blood pumping out as the stranger drank it down. Then, as the blood flow ceased, the stranger leaned back, his blood-stained mouth open, his sharp fangs visible in the moonlight as he keened a small cry, like a bird into the night sky.

'Oh my god,' Richard fell back upon the grass, his hand moving to his mouth. 'I think I'm gonna . . .' he turned to the side, retching, his empty stomach heaving.

Eventually it passed, and he looked back up at Mister Growly.

'It's true,' he whispered. 'He's a vampire.'

'Yes.'

'But why does he want my brother?'

Mister Growly shrugged. 'He cannot travel by daylight, so he most likely needs some kind of thrall to do his bidding. You know, someone to find his next victim so that Orlok doesn't need to do all that boring stalking work when the sun comes down.'

'Mister Bitey makes my brother find his victims? How can I stop it?'

'You have to break the connection,' Mister Growly rose now, moving out of the park. 'You need to stop Orlok - I mean Mister Bitey.'

Richard looked back across the park as a sudden screech echoed across it. Beside the bench, Mister Bitey had now moved to the girl and, as she screamed in both fear and agony he sank his teeth into her throat, pulling at it like a dog worrying a rubber toy. Richard looked away, tears running down his face.

'She was frozen,' he muttered. 'How could she scream?'

'Because he likes them to scream,' Mister Growly replied, leading Richard out of the park. 'Come on, lad. Let's get you home.'

'We should call the police,' Richard looked back to the park as he spoke. 'Perhaps it's not too late . . .'

Mister Growly shook his head.

'The police can't handle this. You saw what happened. They're gone, lad. The best thing you can do is make sure that nobody else suffers their fate.'

Richard nodded, as a vision of Mister Bitey

sinking his teeth into Kevin's throat came into his head.

'I'll help,' he said. 'What do I do?'

Mister Growly told him.

It was morning when Richard saw Kevin next. He'd arrived home after Kevin had gone to bed, and by the time he'd finished being chastised by his parents for not contacting them, for not coming immediately home, for missing dinner, in fact for about half a dozen different things, he was too tired to do anything else. The events of the evening had both scarred and drained him, and he spent a restless night trying to sleep, hounded by nightmares where shadowed vampires attacked him in the dark. Several times he woke in a cold sweat, and when the sun rose, it was with a weary resignation that Richard greeted it, walking down the stairs to face his brother, and the imaginary friend that seemed oh, so real.

'I need to talk to you,' he said simply, sitting down on the carpet in front of Kevin, currently playing cars once more with a small metal truck. Kevin looked up, his eyes hooded and suspicious.

'I've not done anything,' he replied. 'It wasn't me.'

'Not you,' Richard replied, feeling the wave of fear run down his spine as he spoke the next words. 'I mean Mister Bitey.'

He looked up at the window, the sun streaming through it.

'I mean, I assume he's around? It's not like he has anything else to do right now, right?'

Kevin's eyes took on a sly look, as the

slightest hint of a smile appeared on his lips.

'Mister Bitey wants to know why you want to speak to him,' he said. 'He wants to know why you have interest in an imaginary friend.'

'Because I want him to leave my brother alone,' Richard leaned forwards. 'And I know you're not imaginary . . . Orlok.'

The reaction was astounding. Kevin jerked back as if stung, his eyes widening as he looked around in fear.

'Mister Bitey isn't happy!' he cried out.

'Oh I bet he isn't,' Richard replied. 'But I'll make it easier for him to regain his smile, okay? Tell him I want to meet him. Midnight, where he ate the boy and the girl last night.'

Kevin paused, as if listening to a secret voice.

'Why?' he asked.

'Because I want him to leave you alone, Kevin. I want to offer him a better deal.'

Kevin sat still for a moment, his eyes unfocused. Eventually they looked at Richard.

'Deal,' he said.

Richard smiled, rising from the carpet.

'See you there then,' he said as he turned and walked away.

But even though his voice was relaxed, inside he was far from it. All he hoped was that Mister Growly's plan worked. Because if it didn't, there was a very strong chance that after midnight, Richard wouldn't be coming home.

'I don't think he's coming,' Richard muttered, looking around the park. Mister Growly, leaning against a swing checked his watch.

'It's not midnight yet. Will you please relax?'

Richard sighed and sat back down on the bench. It hadn't been difficult to leave the house, as his bedroom window looked out onto the garage roof and it had just been a matter of ensuring that the dustbin was beside the back wall to break the drop. Once out, it was a brisk walk to the park and the tweed jacketed old man who waited there.

Faintly, Richard heard the bells of St Seward's chime the hour. Midnight. Resisting the urge to shudder, Richard stared around the park, looking for any sign of Mister Bitey.

'Behind you.'

The voice took Richard by surprise, and as he spun around to face the shadowed man behind him, he noted that Mister Growly had already disappeared. He was alone in the park as Mister Bitey grabbed him by the lapel of his jacket.

'Kevin's brother,' he hissed. 'Won't be missed, from what I've seen.'

'I want you to leave my brother alone!' Richard cried out, the terror in his voice raising it by an octave. 'I don't want him to be your . . . your *Froll* anymore.'

Mister Bitey stared down at Richard, his eyes rising in surprise as his pale face caught the lamp light.

'Froll?' he whispered. 'Do you mean Thrall?'

'Whatever!' Richard yelled. 'I'm not gonna let you use him!'

And with that he pulled a small glass spice jar out of his pocket, flipping the plastic lid open with his thumb as he threw the contents over the vampire in front of him. Mister Bitey screamed in pain as the granules of salt hit his face, dropping

Richard as he used his cloak to brush them away.

'What did you do?' he screamed as he grabbed the jar, reading the label. 'Garlic granules with parsley? I should kill you for this!'

'You gotta catch me first,' Richard turned and, getting to his feet he sprinted away from the burned and now furious vampire. He managed five feet before he felt his leg caught in Mister Bitey's grasp, and the weightlessness of being thrown across the park by the vampire's fearsome strength. It was a good fifteen, twenty feet before he landed in a heap beside the roundabout, screaming out at a possibly sprained ankle.

In front of him Mister Bitey stalked towards him, his face still smoking where the spice had struck.

'Now you die,' he hissed.

Richard forced a smile through his grimace of pain.

'Not yet,' he gasped. 'First you meet *my* imaginary friend.'

Mister Bitey paused, and that was all it took. With a yelp of triumph, Mister Growly burst through the trees, charging into the vampire, sending him flying. Gone was the tweed coat – now the werewolf was as Richard remembered, apart from some greyer fur. He was fast, vicious, feral and before Mister Bitey could react Mister Growly had already scored vicious wounds upon his body. But then the surprise was over, and Mister Bitey managed to throw Mister Growly aside, gaining a few seconds of valuable time to gather his wits before the werewolf was upon him once more.

The two sides were evenly matched. Mister Growly bit hard and true, but Mister Bitey gave as good as he received, taking chunks out of the old werewolf's hide, spitting them aside as he wrenched bones and tore muscles. Even with the sprained ankle, Richard knew that he had to help somehow and, rummaging through his jacket, he found the other item that he had brought with him.

A plastic sports bottle.

'Hey, Bitey,' he shouted as the vampire once more threw the werewolf aside. 'You're looking rough. Want a drink? It's isotonic.'

'The only drink I want is your blood,' Mister Bitey hissed as he limped towards Richard, waving a hand.

Richard suddenly realised with horror that he couldn't move a muscle. The same trick that had been played on the two teenagers the night before was now being played on him. Mister Bitey smiled as the realisation hit his victim's eyes.

'Yes,' he said, moving ever closer. 'The game is over. Now watch as I drink you dry –'

The remainder of the line turned into a yelp of pain and anger as Mister Growly, now hideously mangled yet still fighting managed to clamp his teeth onto Mister Bitey's ankle. As the vampire yelled, his mental grasp over Richard diminished enough for the young boy to grip hard on the bottle, forcing the liquid out, squirting it directly into the vampire's eyes.

'Holy water,' he said, as Mister Bitey staggered back, his face bubbling, melting off as he desperately tried to keep it in place with his hands.

Mister Growly, now back on his feet, leapt at the vampire, taking Mister Bitey's throat out with a savage growl. The headless body of Mister Bitey fell to the floor, the holy water still burning through the skin.

Richard leaned back, staring at the sky.

'Done,' he whispered.

It was the lapping sound that made him look back down. Mister Growly was drinking the blood out from Mister Bitey's neck, his fangs and fur red with the liquid. His black eyes were shining and his lustrous brown fur had lost all trace of grey.

'Mister Growly?' was all that Richard could whisper.

The werewolf paused his drinking, looking over to the boy.

'For years I have wanted this,' he growled. 'To have the immortality of a vampire mixed with the strength of a werewolf! I can rule everything! Kill everyone!'

Richard shook his head.

'But you're good!' he whispered. 'You helped me . . .'

Mister Growly started to laugh, a bitter, feral growl of amusement that terrified Richard.

'Fodder. You were nothing more than a meatshield.'

Richard stared at Mister Growly. Finally the memories returned, of the imaginary friend of his youth. The funny, clever dog in the jeans with the red Converse trainers who kept him safe.

'Please,' he whispered as Mister Growly lapped up the last of the blood. 'Please, don't kill me.'

'You want me to let you go?' Mister Growly turned to face the boy, his smile a razor sharp mass of teeth.

'Please . . .'

'You want me to be a *good* dog? Just like old times?'

'Yes . . .'

'Say it,' Mister Growly moved ever closer to Richard, the blood of Mister Bitey all over his muzzle.

'Please, please be a good dog . . .'

Mister Growly *wasn't.*

***Tony Lee** is a #1 New York Times Bestselling author of graphic novels, audio dramas and screenplays that include* Doctor Who, Spider Man *and* Pride and Prejudice and Zombies. *A member of the Society for over five years, he lives with his wife Tracy where he spends his days writing fantastical situations aimed at hurting fantastical characters. A council member of the Sherlock Holmes Society of London, he has yet to write the Sherlock Holmes / Jonathan Harker team-up he's dreamed of since childhood. His website is www.tonylee.co.uk*

A WOMAN'S LIFE IS IN HER BAG
Laura Miller

Her toes had welcomed the feel of the soft carpet beneath them, her high strappy sandals abandoned on the stairs beside her. She rubbed the sole of one foot: bloody shoes. They looked good but she was now unused to wearing them. She moved them to the stair beneath those she sat on. There were no waitresses left in the room she had just exited, but the last thing she needed was someone tripping over the things.

She could see, further down the corridor ahead of her, that the queue for the cloakroom was still long. Ray's blond head could be glimpsed above the others. He was tall, and she knew Debbie would be hanging from his arm giggling, the remains of her glass of champagne resting against the breast of his jacket. There was an almost comical disparity in their heights but otherwise they were the perfect couple.

Two years on even she had to admit it was time, as her mother had started to insist more regularly, to 'move on'. A month previously she had removed her wedding ring then, paranoid that she might be burgled whilst at work, she had taped it to the back of the headboard of what had been their marital bed. Her finger still looked bare. Chris sighed, grabbed a pack of cigarettes from her bag, pulled one out and lit it.

Having told Debbie and Ray that she felt able to go out for an evening, they had been careful about her re-entry into social life. Chris recognised their consideration. Glitzy enough, with dancing, not too stuffy and a large enough percentage of the cover price for the ticket going to charity to ensure that Chris was less likely to back out at the last minute. A mix of couples and singles, Chris realised that her in-laws' secret hope was that she would meet someone, a replacement for the irreplaceable. She'd taken a long drag on her cigarette.

It had been a themed party above a glitzy Soho restaurant; themes were good, providing material for otherwise meagre conversations: 'great outfit, what a cool idea . . .'

The charity had been to help save some animal, not to assist with any human frailty or disease. Although Simon had not been frail at all, his aneurism had been the cruel biological equivalent to an act of God. Nature was not cruel, though: it just was. She shivered; someone had opened a window in the room behind her to clear the air of the smell of stale perfume, cigarette smoke and spilt champagne.

The theme had been described as 'The Age of Glamour', but perhaps because *The Great Gatsby* was showing in London's cinemas the party had been full of ersatz flappers. Chris, on entering, had been momentarily proud of her thirties themed outfit. A long bias cut dress in a mint green complimented a figure that had been diminished by grief and her pale brown hair was pinned up in a soft roll behind the nape of her neck. She looked more Mitford than Hollywood but had enjoyed a brief alien lurch of pleasure on examining herself in the mirror before leaving.

Now, however, she felt tawdry: she had danced, hung on some man's arm disinterestedly before rapidly drinking perhaps one glass too many of champagne. What had her mother always said? 'Never be the last to leave a party'. Chris had ruminated on what terrible fate could befall you if you did, but perhaps now she had an inkling. She felt totally alone and completely singular sitting on the stair at the entrance to that now silent room, her silver sandals set at her feet like an offering. She looked back into the room behind her: single stack of chairs, one champagne bottle leaning against the wall, one glass beside it, one trestle table, a bag.

The bag was jammed behind the rear leg of the table. Chris could picture what had happened earlier that evening. Some girl had wanted to dance and stowed her bag there. Drunkenness, fatigue or romance had intervened and she had forgotten it. Someone was going to have a tedious ending to her evening.

Chris pulled herself up from the stair, grabbed her sandals and padded across the empty room to retrieve it. Tugging it from its hiding place she examined it: Yves St Laurent, a hard-cased snap evening bag with no chain. Heavy and encrusted with crystals, it caught the light from the mirror ball rotating dolefully in the middle of the empty room and threw them back into her face. It was expensive and whoever had left it had, like Chris, made the decision to reference the thirties. She was aware guiltily that the civilised response was to simply find her friends and hand the bag over to the cloakroom attendants. But the bag was expensive and unusual; the clasp opened with a loud snap.

Chris examined the contents. A set of keys and a large roll of what looked like £50 banknotes fastened with a thick grubby elastic band. Not in a purse, the utilitarian nature of storing what was obviously a large amount of money had made her feel instinctively wary. They were in Soho – had she found the bag of a high-class escort girl?

The rest of the contents were no more comforting, two or three small plastic tubs of prescription drugs. Chris read the labels but didn't recognise the drugs; the name of the patient was too faint to be clear. Other items included a set of keys, a Chanel lipstick, a condom and also a familiar item of jewellery. It was a 'SOS' bracelet identical in design to the one her mother wore to alert others of her allergies. Turning it over in her hand, Chris could see this one was gold and hallmarked. She picked the cover open with a glittery varnished nail then pulled out and read the typewritten message on the small piece of paper it contained: 'in case of fit, medication on person. Call Dr. Alistair McMonahon'. A London telephone number followed.

The final article in the bag was a small card case that Chris also opened. It contained several small identical cards plainly engraved 'Solange Adams, Solicitor, Rilke and Moore', followed by another 01 telephone number. So, thought Chris wryly, not quite the kind of solicitation she had expected. She replaced the bag's contents, snapped it shut, put her sandals back on and crossed the empty room towards the now diminished queue for the cloakroom.

Taking her coat from Ray, Chris explained 'I'm going to ring the work number, leave a message so the poor woman knows her stuff is safe, then drop it into Savile Row Police Station.'

Debbie looked concerned. 'If she needs the medicine urgently she isn't going to be able to collect it from a closed restaurant is she?'

'It's ok, I'll hail a cab in Piccadilly,' clarified Chris. Air kissing her friends goodbye, she made her way down to the pay phone booth in the lobby of the restaurant. She retrieved a card from the bag and rang the number upon it. Abruptly, the call was answered, a soft female voice.

'Hello, this is Solange Adams.'

'Oh,' said Chris, wrong footed. 'I found your bag at Kettner's. I mean, I have your bag, I am dropping it off at the police station.'

'No,' the woman interrupted. 'I really need the medication'.

'Ah,' replied Chris. 'I didn't expect to get an answer.'

There was a pause on the end of the line. Then the woman replied, more warmly, 'I am so relieved someone nice and honest found it. I was becoming desperate: my door keys are in the bag and my office, well, it is open all night. It's in the West End; could I come and pick the bag up off you? I have a vascular condition and I need to take those pills before the morning, it would only be fifteen minutes and you'd be a lifesaver. I'll arrange a cab to take you home to wherever you need to be.'

Chris paused – Solange could as easily pick up the bag from the police station.

'Okay,' Chris answered, 'where?'

'Cross Passage, do you know it, runs behind St James?'

Cross Passage? Chris did know it; during the day it functioned as a convenient short cut and contained several small sandwich shops servicing local office workers. It was not a dangerous part of town but would be dark and empty at this time of night. She checked her watch: 1am.

Solange seemed to sense her hesitation. 'It's quiet, I know, but,' she paused, 'there's a lot of money in the bag, I had to look after the takings from a friend's event earlier in the evening and was planning to pop them in the work safe. Sadly I drank a little too much. I don't want to open the bag in a crowded place.'

Chris assented and put the phone down, her sandals were digging into her feet and she felt very weary. Simpler to just tolerate the ten-minute walk and hand the bag, which was beginning to feel like a burden, over to its rightful owner.

Fifteen minutes later as Chris turned into Cross Passage it started to rain lightly and she pulled her coat more tightly around her. Great – her feet were going to be blistered and wet. The bag was sharp and awkward to carry, she could see why Solange had discarded it: a beautiful thing but not comfortable. She wandered what kind of woman would choose it and imagined someone slightly exotic: Solange was hardly a common English name. There didn't seem to be anyone around yet and Chris shivered involuntarily.

A few minutes passed and she heard footsteps as two figures turned in from the Pall Mall end of the passage. One waved and shouted 'Don't worry, I'm Solange and this is Michael, a security guard from the Office. He is here to guard us against footpads.' Chris recalled thinking that 'footpads' was a curiously antiquated term.

As Michael stepped forward into the light, she saw that he was wearing a uniform. He was tall, unsmiling and good looking. Solange was initially disappointing; a petite woman no taller than five foot, blonde hair scraped back from a sharp, intelligent face. Her clothes were expensive: she was wearing what looked like a purple jumpsuit, very high heels and was wrapped in a large fur stole, possibly mink. Unconcerned by the rain, her face was wet with raindrops. She reminded Chris of one of her father's netsuke, small and contained. Surely she hadn't worn that fur to the wildlife charity party?

Solange smiled at Chris gratefully and extended her hand towards her bag. The smile altered her face completely and Chris noticed large, round, pale blue eyes. It was a warm smile and communicated amusement rather than relief.

'Can I have your address?' said Solange taking the bag. 'I'd love to be able to thank you properly; you really have saved my life and do let me pay for your cab home. I have been so inconvenient.'

Chris pulled her diary out of her bag,

scribbled her address on a page and tore it out, passing it to Solange. She demurred on the cab front. She really was exhausted, her feet hurt and the champagne she had consumed earlier made her stomach sting. She really couldn't do any of it anymore, any of that kind of night any more. She said 'Goodbye, glad you got it back safely,' and turned away, back in the direction of Piccadilly.

Within the following few minutes, and it was, she knew, a matter of minutes, something hit her hard on the back of the head, probably Michael's fist and she fell. Her foot twisted on her high heels and she recalled thinking, faintly ridiculously, that she would never wear them again. She was caught before she fell and then remembered hearing, just before completely blacking out, the single word: 'grief'.

She eventually came around in University College Hospital's Intensive Care ward. Naturally the papers had a field day: 'Tragic young widow mauled in Mayfair' being amongst the least sensational mastheads of the day. By the time she had recovered sufficiently to go home, a couple of IRA bombings, strike threats and a general election had blessedly moved her from the public consciousness.

The police had discovered that Solange Adams, Rilke and Moore Solicitors and Dr. McMahon were fictitious. The telephone number Chris had called belonged to The New Piccadilly Café. Its proprietor, Mr Marini, recalled a woman resembling Solange's description and agreed that a customer might have picked up his phone from the wall without being noticed - it was always busy and noisy that late on a Saturday night. Other than this, he could not help. Chris herself had been discovered lying in a pool of blood at 2 am by a drunken reveller staggering into the passage to relieve himself.

Her survival had been near miraculous – Chris recalled, however, that survival had not really been a fair description of her state in the months following the attack. Her neck was ravaged, with a large vicious series of cuts that had mangled and congealed into a livid scar, which smarted each time she moved her neck.

Worse was a continued sense of foreboding only enhanced by constant fatigue. When able to sleep, she awoke un-refreshed and with the sense of having had terrible dreams she could not recall. She shook uncontrollably when lifting a glass and felt merely a slow, barely repressed fury with the family and friends who crowded around her less and less as the months passed. Post-traumatic stress they would call it now.

The only positive was a blunting of her grief. Her attackers were not traced and the only conclusion the authorities could tentatively suggest was that they had been under the 'influence of drugs', the 20th century version of blaming 'an escaped lunatic'. This not even half-life had continued for six months, her mother's death had barely registered, and by the summer, 'recluse' was a term that really could have been applied to her without reservation. She left the house only to collect the library books that proved the only balm to sleepless nights and buy food she seldom ate.

It was upon returning from the local library in early September that Chris had found them there. The moment she turned into her road she experienced a preternatural feeling of danger that even the Valium could not prevent. As she turned the key in the lock, every hair left on the unscarred portion of her neck had stood up.

They were there – Michael sat on her sofa looking at her. Solange, impeccable in a long white cotton dress was examining the books untidily heaped onto a battered table.

'Good books, clever books,' she said, turning to Chris.

Chris could only stand there, a plastic bag of tattered books in one hand, her key still in the other. She felt like a small animal that had just blundered into some predator's den. She recalled the page in the notebook with her address.

Solange looked at her in amusement. 'I said we'd come back to thank you.'

Chris initially thought, unimaginatively she now felt, that they had come back to kill her because she might remember something. But deep from somewhere within, she felt that most petty of emotions: indignation.

'Why are you doing this to me?' she enquired hoarsely.

Solange frowned slightly. 'Because we had to, and grief tastes so exquisite, we couldn't stop when we should have. I'm sorry.'

Chris must have looked confused.

'We'd just end it,' explained Solange, 'but you were so honest, and after all, we women keep our entire worlds in our bags, don't we? So we will make it better.'

Looking back, the episode was still surreal, but Chris had been so worn down, terror and fatigue so intermingled, that she had not so much as moved or twitched. Even as Solange had grabbed her by the wrists, as Michael clasped her neck, she had remained rooted to the spot. She had dropped her house keys but that stupid bag full of library books had remained clenched in her hand for the whole time.

It hadn't taken long. She would have been treated gently this time. It was, ironically, a bloodless act. She understood now that she was already so far along that something had to be done and yet . . . what they had done was not an act without consequences or lightly undertaken. It would have been easier to push her from a window, in front of a car; anything that damaged her sufficiently to truly finish her off. But they hadn't. She'd never seen them again although they must have watched her flat whilst she was, for want of a better word, asleep.

She'd awoken, her scars gone, her head clear, a long letter to her in a sprawling script placed under a framed wedding photograph and several thousand pounds in her bank account. She had taken notice of that letter, sold up, taken herself to America and come to terms with her bizarre folkloric situation in a cabin near Oja, California, where strangeness was virtually compulsory amongst its residents.

Of course she had revisited London several times: she'd felt a compelling need to visit Simon's grave in the scrubby Streatham graveyard in which he'd been interred. She'd renewed the plot rental, claiming to be his niece. It felt safer now and she had rented a large house in one of Mayfair's quieter spots. But until now she had not returned to Kettner's.

The party was winding down and although the venue had been comprehensively and not very sympathetically refurbished, it still felt familiar. The floor was no longer carpeted and this event was not for charity; perhaps that animal had become extinct, rather as she had. This was a 'burlesque' cabaret. Another *Great Gatsby* film was on the horizon and again flappers predominated. To her eyes, the High Street versions were tawdry and cheaply embellished. She favoured vintage clothing; she enjoyed being cloaked by the scent of a garment's previous owners. The girls were pretty, however, and had enjoyed 'vamping' it up in cheap lace and kohled eyes.

One of the prettiest was with Scott. She, of course, could hear his quiet Californian voice full of reserve and halting charm within the hubbub of the room. The girl would imagine she was on the cusp of a new relationship with this polite, wealthy, fey and young American who seemed to really understand her. She was unaware that the evening would come to a sickening, traumatic end in a police station, bleeding and incoherent. It was unkind but efficient and the victim would come to no real harm, physically at least. For a predator this was benevolent, although Chris often felt that 'parasite' was a more accurate description of their condition.

She'd met Scott in the 80s when he had been on a College graduation drinking tour with his classmates in Tijuana. Softly spoken, preppy and blonde. His reluctance to indulge in frat house antics had made it easy to separate him from his classmates. It was assumed he'd befallen a terrible fate in the desert, and in a sense he had. Chris heard the girl laugh at one of Scott's quips. He turned and caught her eye and she shook her head; he raised an eyebrow and shrugged. Excusing himself, he headed towards the bar. Chris knew he would collect her fur and his coat and wait for her outside.

Her eyes skirted around the rapidly emptying room. In one corner was a nest of sofas; on one a young man was sprawled, half asleep. Chris knew he would instinctively awake if she went too close, so she chose the other. Chris's clutch bag was Alexander McQueen: a sequinned leopard print design with a jewelled knuckle-duster clasp; not this season but it had cost more than most of these partygoers' monthly salaries. Its contents: a mobile phone, a Vuitton purse full of cash and three Adrenaline Epipens.

Chris bent down and in one swift unseen movement jammed it between the sofa and the wall, ensuring it could be partially seen. She left swiftly. It had started to rain softly; she lit the cigarette she had longed to smoke all night. Scott slipped his arm through hers and they headed off to the Bar Italia to wait . . .

Laura Miller *is a Londoner. She obtained her bachelor degree in History of Art from the University of Cambridge and her Masters degree in Informatics from City University. She lived for* *several years in central Japan, and has lectured on Japanese demons and demon hunters. More recent research has been on the visual role of books in modern western art. An occasional reviewer, journalist and illustrator, she has a long and abiding interest in all things Gothic.*

THE INNER SPECTRUM
Barry McCann

She failed to notice them at first. Freshly risen from bed, Pandora stood before the dressing mirror, busily grooming herself. Craning her head to back brush, she spotted two small wounds on the side of her neck. Putting her hand upon the marks, they felt quite pronounced, though numb. Little wonder she was unaware of their presence before the mirror alerted her. Proceeding to dress, Pandora realised she still felt fatigued despite a full night's sleep. Fully clothed, she rubbed her hand over the wounds again and wondered about consulting the local physician. Her father would certainly insist on it. But then, she was all he had left in life, and he all she had.

Pandora had married young; but then came the Great War from which her husband had failed to return. Her mother had died some years earlier and her grieving father, a rector with the Church of England, accepted an incumbency in the Cornish village of Petra Gos, a remote community presently in the cradle of autumnal change. The widowed Pandora joined him there and dedicated herself to looking after parish affairs along with their resident housekeeper, Janet. Though earning some admirers, she kept herself dutiful and lived in hope that her missing husband would walk back into her life one day.

'Dear God. What manner of creature made those?' Her father exclaimed upon being showed the mysterious marks.

'Creature?' she queried.

'Those are bite marks, made by an animal. I'm sending for Doctor Carmichael.'

'Oh, father – he's a busy man. And I am sure they will heal.'

The rector shook his head. 'We don't know what bit you or if it could be carrying infection. Better to be cautious.'

Pandora realised the wisdom of her father's words and the village doctor was around in no time. He examined the wounds with deep curiosity and bemusement, as her father and housekeeper looked on. He then checked Pandora's eyes and sat back.

'Was there any trace of blood? On your pillow, perhaps?'

'None at all,' Pandora replied. 'Why?'

'Because there is indication you have lost some. I suspect it was taken by whatever bit you.'

'A blood sucker!' her father exclaimed. 'What demon has Satan sent here?'

The doctor shook his head, as he retrieved a bottle and some cotton wool from his bag. 'There is a species of bat that lives on blood. They are indigenous to South America, but one could have escaped from a menagerie and found its way here.' He soaked the wool with the disinfectant mixture and dabbed it on Pandora's wounds.

'Mind you, this must be a large specimen given the size of these wounds. That's quite a large gap between the incisors,' he replaced the bottle and closed his bag, then asked Pandora: 'Did you sleep with your window open last night?'

'Yes. I usually do.'

'Well, keep it closed tonight. Having found a source of nourishment, it may return.'

He then looked up at the rector and the housekeeper. 'I think we had better do a thorough search of this young lady's room. Just in case something has secreted itself.'

Pandora remained downstairs while the others examined her bed chamber. Satisfied that nothing was hiding in there, the three returned to the lounge.

'Well, there are no uninvited visitors there now,' announced the doctor. 'So a rest for you, young lady. And keep your window closed tonight.'

Pandora followed his orders and had a trouble free night. The wounds were also healing with no sign of infection and both she and her father were confident that the incident was closed. But the night following saw the case suddenly reopened.

It was in the early hours that she stirred from a vivid dream. One in which her husband appeared at the end of her bed, looking down upon her while holding up an ornate mask around his eyes and quietly saying 'In the eye of past presence, life awaits on either side.' Looking up, she opened her arms, lamenting 'Send me an angel.' Her husband slowly moved to the bedside with eyes fixed upon her through the frame of the mask. He then lowered it, revealing his face in full, and came down upon her in a passionate embrace.

It was then Pandora woke, her eyes adjusting to the empty darkness that first met them. But her frame still registered the sensation of somebody partially lying upon her torso, and a wet feeling on the side of her neck.

Turning her head, something jumped back and stood upright in the dark. Her eyes tried to make sense of the figure, the dim moonlight that shone through the window revealing the silhouette of a human head, a woman by the length of its hair. It also highlighted two further features: a pair of wide, bloodshot eyes staring down and an open mouth revealing bloodstained teeth, two of which were sharp, protruding fangs. Pandora screamed and the figure shot deep into the darker recess of the room. It was not long before her father came bursting into the room, closely followed by Janet, both in their night clothes. He found his daughter sat upright in bed, rubbing her neck in shock. As Janet lit the bedside candle, he sat on the bed and gently pulled away Pandora's hand to reveal fresh wounds.

'Dear God. It's struck again!' he pronounced.

The doctor arrived first thing next morning and repeated his examination with her father and Janet in attendance. He shook his head, declaring, 'Exactly the same as before.' He then looked up at the pair.

'And the windows were shut?'

'Aye, sir.' Janet replied. 'Saw to that myself. And I have checked the room for any sign of . . . well, anything.'

'There was someone there last night!'

Pandora pleaded once again. 'I saw her. And her teeth. She must have bit me!'

'You said yourself you were just awakening,' the doctor insisted. 'You were coming out of a dream.'

The rector pointed in the direction of his daughter's neck. 'You're still not telling me that is the work of a bat. Those wounds are too big and I know what the culprit is likely to be.'

Doctor Carmichael sighed. 'I take it you are implying a human vampire. Rector Newman, we are both men of reason and they are the stuff of penny dreadfuls.'

The rector nodded his head. 'Normally I would agree, but I am also a man of God. And as such, I cannot deny the possible work of Satan.'

Doctor Carmichael looked back at Pandora. 'There could be other explanations that have simply not occurred to us,' he stood up, picking up his bag and continued, 'You take whatever precautions you think best. Meanwhile I shall make enquiries. See if there is an escaped lunatic in the area. It could be as simple as that.'

As Janet escorted the doctor out, Rector Newman turned to his daughter, producing a crucifix on a chain.

'Wear this at all times from now on, my child. The doctor may well be right, but until we know, it is better we assume the worst and act accordingly.' He smiled happily as Pandora accepted the trinket and placed it around her neck.

Night was falling when Doctor Carmichael unexpectedly returned, accompanied by two of the local village men. All three wore grim looks on their faces. Janet ushered them into the parlour, where they were joined by Rector Newman and Pandora.

'You know Nick and Brian,' the doctor confirmed. 'They came to see me, so I brought them straight over.' He glanced accusingly at Janet, adding, 'Someone talked in the village this afternoon.'

Janet looked at her employer in resignation. 'I had to tell them, sir. If there is something dangerous in the parish, they have a right to know. Protect their families.'

'Aye, that's right,' Nick piped up first. 'We should have been told from the start. Before it come for our wives and children!'

'We don't even know what it is,' the rector explained.

'We do!' Brian declared. 'There's a tale that, centuries ago, a ship ran aground at Stepper's Point near Padstow. It come from the Black Sea and was carrying something.' He momentarily hesitated before continuing, 'Something that escaped and found its way inland. To this village.'

'It fed on human blood.' Nick continued. 'Folk were waking up to find bites on their necks and blood lost. Worse still, some didn't wake up at all. Eventually, a Jesuit priest was brought in to hold a midnight exorcism at graveyard, as it was reckoned that's where it took refuge. The attacks then stopped.'

'Was this attacker ever seen?' the sceptical doctor enquired.

'No. That were its trick. 'Tis said it could not be seen with human eye, as it weren't human.'

'Or it hid in the shroud of darkness as vampires are said to do,' Rector Newman suggested.

Doctor Carmichael shook his head. ‘Oh, come on. It’s just a story,’ he reasoned. ‘You folk are full of such tales.’

‘Aye, and we know they’re mostly fancies,’ Brian continued, before leaning forward towards the rector. ‘But that don’t mean they all are.’

Rector Newman looked at the doctor, commenting, ‘I share your wariness of local superstition. But with no other explanation we have to consider the possibility at least.’

Doctor Carmichael quietly nodded and conceded. ‘All right. I’ll go along with the possibility. Until we discover the truth, that is.’

Nick shook the rector’s hand. ‘Thank you, pastor. I had faith we could count on you.’

‘But I’m no papist. This is the church of King James. I have never done an exorcism.’

‘If it’s come back, then exorcism alone is no good. We need to hunt it down and banish it forever this time.’ Brian murmured in agreement and Nick continued.

‘And it must be done this very night! We’ll round up our families and put them in village hall. The rest of us will join you and we‘ll go to the cemetery. Finds its lair and we‘ll find it!’

The Rector gave a concerned glance at Pandora. ‘But, my daughter . . .’

‘Some of the lads will surround your house. Nothing will get past them.’

Pandora then spoke. ‘You must do your duty, Father.’

‘The lads will protect her,’ Brian chimed in.

‘And I will stay in her room tonight. I can sleep in a chair,’ added Janet.

Evening fell and a dozen or so of the local men arrived at the Rectory, led by the doctor. The rector was in his full vestments, ready to receive them as Janet opened the door and the group filed in. They were armed with knives and scythes, much to the rector's discomfort. But he had to go along.

The group watched as he bid his daughter goodnight, adding 'You are still wearing the crucifix?'

'Yes. God go with you, father.'

'And God be with you.' With that, he turned and the vigilante group parted as he walked forward and took his place at the front, declaring 'Now, my brothers. Let us root out this evil and pray for the Lord's blessing in our holy task.'

'We shall begin in the graveyard,' Doctor Carmichael added. 'If the myths are true, sacred earth is the traditional resting place for creatures of this nature.'

The group departed and Pandora watched through the parlour window as they headed in the direction of the village cemetery. Her father led them, holding up a bible against his chest and praying aloud. As they disappeared into the night, she turned her head to another part of the grounds where two more armed men stood on guard duty. They gave her a reassuring wave and Pandora felt secure. With nothing else to be done now, she decided to retire. She checked again through her bedroom window and one of the men was directly below, smoking a cigarette as he kept watch. She turned as the housekeeper entered the room, carrying a chair which she placed down.

'That is really kind of you, Janet. But I will

be fine, really.'

'I'll feel better being in here with you, my dear. Don't want to take any more chances.'

Pandora let out a laugh. 'I've probably got more guarding me than the crown jewels. We could have just joined the others at the village hall.'

Janet smiled and added, 'Well, you get yourself ready for bed while I go down and make us a cup of hot milk.'

'Thank you, Janet.'

With that, the housekeeper departed and Pandora began to undress.

Having changed into her nightgown, Pandora went over to the mirror to groom her hair in the candlelight, its reflection casting even greater illumination. Raising the brush to her fringe and craning her neck back, she noticed the two wounds were no longer there. Lowering the brush, she quickly raised her other hand to her neck and could still feel them. Staring carefully in the mirror, she slowly removed her hand to reveal perfect, unblemished flesh. She dropped the brush and felt with both hands, and they still registered the puncture remarks. Pandora was so confused that, at first, she was slow to notice another anomaly about her reflection. It was smiling back at her.

Pandora instinctively stepped back a few paces while her reflection remained still, the corners of its smile curling down with a sinister ambiance. She backed away further, right up against the dressing table as the reflection moved forward and stepped out of the mirror, like someone emerging through a waterfall from behind.

As the figure pulled out from the glass, its frame refracted into a fuller dimension. The smiling expression turned sardonic as it approached Pandora and spoke with her voice. 'They seek out what should be sought within.'

Pandora bent backward over the dresser, pulling the crucifix out from under her nightdress and holding it up to ward off her predator. But the doppelganger came right up and brushed it aside.

'I'm afraid that part is superstition,' the figure commented as it put its hands on her shoulders in a caressing fashion. Pandora gasped as its lips parted, revealing a pair of sharp, canine like fangs.

'But 'tis true we cast no reflection,' it intoned, gently brushing Pandora's cheek. 'For we *are* reflection. The perfect sanctuary.'

The double grabbed Pandora by the hair and pulled her head sideways down. With neck exposed, its fangs sank into the ready-made wounds to feast for the third and final time.

Barry McCann *is a published writer, editor, speaker and broadcaster. He has been editor of the art & literature journal* Parnassus *for MENSA International since **1998** and regularly appears on BBC Radio Cumbria as their 'Folklore Correspondent', having previously enjoyed a writer in residence slot on BBC Radio Lancashire. He recently hosted at the Hastings Queen of Horror Festival in honour of Ingrid Pitt, during which he made his acting debut with Carole Cleveland and Damien Thomas. Barry has also won the accolade of being turned into a Blackpool illumination, which he considers his crowning achievement.*

MORE FUN THAN A VAMPIRE-HUNTING KIT
Gail-Nina Anderson

'I'm so glad you're here, dear,' said Mrs Cornwell. 'We've got a little domestic problem you might be able to solve.'

Justin suppressed the sigh that, along with a mouthful of whiskey-soaked fruitcake threatened to rise to his lips. Why did his grandmother always assume that, because he was male, he could unblock sinks, mend gutterings and re-attach sofa legs? He had no bent for the mechanical, no yearning towards the occult universe of plumbing and quite definitely no desire to poke around in anyone's u-bend.

And come to that, why did his grandmother invariably find a way to introduce alcohol into the ritual of afternoon tea? He was barely a drinker at the best of times, and at four o'clock in the afternoon all he usually looked forward to was a decaff latte and a few amusing Tweets. Justin was a cerebral young man, but not detached from the modern world – oh no, far from it. His was a universe of the brain and the computer. He loved the way that arcane ideas were not only communicated, but actively shaped by this means of transmission.

Nervously he crumbled his fruitcake (as a safe alternative to eating or even sniffing it) and adjusted his rather emphatic dark-rimmed spectacles.

'Are they new, dear? They make you look awfully studious.'

'Geek chic,' piped up Auntie Mary, as she reached for a second slice of cake.

Auntie Mary had been a part of Justin's life for as long as he could remember, though she definitely wasn't his aunt. Indeed, he suspected she wasn't related to anyone, or at least to anyone who would admit it. She had inexplicably been his grandmother's best friend for decades. He recalled her from his childhood years, with tightly permed black hair, wraparound floral pinnie and the fearsome false teeth that had frightened him as a boy. The hair was now grey and the apron had been replaced by an enormous cardigan, apparently knitted on tent poles. He averted his eyes from the teeth.

'That's what they call it, Maureen – geek chic,' his grandmother's friend nodded sagely. 'Just like Clark Kent – or do I mean Clark Gable? Oh no – Gregory Peck, that's the one!'

He was helpless against this cascade of mad word association, but his grandmother cut effortlessly across her friend, with a determination born from years of practice.

'It's a computer problem – should be right up your street. We're 'silver surfers' you know – it's on the recreation programme.'

He had known – indeed, he'd helped his parents select a computer for his grandmother the previous Christmas. She and Auntie Mary had enrolled in a computer class at the local library, intended as a gentle introduction for senior citizens who didn't have six-year-old grandchildren on hand to teach them the rudiments.

'It was the biscuits that got us hooked at first, of course,' piped up Mary.

'Oh, yes – and the cakes. There's not always much point in baking these days, with no one around to eat it,' she looked pointedly at the mess of Justin's unconsumed fruitcake. 'So the computer class was a blessing – bit of a get-together, tea and buns, you know. But then there was the computer training of course, as well – email and . . .' (a slight hesitation here) '. . . *eBay!*'

Justin had prayed this day would never come. They had discovered eBay.

'We picked that up *straight* away. Just like the little auctions they used to have at the church fete.'

'We've done ever so well – sold a lot of your granddad's bits and pieces. And bought some nice things, too.'

She gestured towards the cushion covers, decorated with crinolined ladies picked out in crewel stitch. Justin had noticed them – could hardly not have done – but had thought the old women might have been taking embroidery classes. But *eBay*, that Aladdin's cave for the unwary . . .

'So have you got yourselves into a dispute, is that it? There are some dodgy characters out there.'

The women exchanged glances of amusement.

'Oh no – you couldn't say we've been cheated or anything. It's just that Mary's gone and bought a ghost.'

This statement didn't provoke so much surprise in Justin as might have been expected. He too had explored the outer reaches of the online market, had seen the 'genuine vampire-hunter kits' for sale, not to mention the various pieces of equipment that allowed you to detect supernatural activity by technological means. But clarification was necessary.

'And were you actually *trying* to buy a ghost at the time,' he found himself asking, 'or did it just come with the cushion covers?'

The women looked at each other with a trace of guilt.

'Well we were really just doing a bit of market research – scoping out the opposition, you might say. It's not that our vampire-hunter's kits haven't been selling well . . .'

Justin closed his eyes.

'Oh yes, love, and there's no great trick to it. A battered old case, a mallet, a couple of wooden stakes that Mr Moorcock makes for us in his woodwork classes. Then you just gussy it up with anything interesting you've got to hand – a bit of stained lace, a faded photo or two, a little prayer book or a scrap of an old letter . . .'

'Anything really, except actual human remains.'

'Ah yes, dear – such a shame about Mr Moorcock's toes. We could have woven such a good story around them, and honestly, now they're off he doesn't have much use for them so . . .'

'Is this Mr Moorcock who does the woodworking classes?' said Justin, visions of carpentry-related accidents flitting horribly across his mind. His grandmother caught his drift at once.

'Oh don't worry Justin – he had them off in the hospital. Apparently he'd danced too much when he was young.' A wistful look of memories briefly recaptured hovered on the faces of both women.

'Anyway, we weren't allowed to sell them and we're getting rather bored with the vampire kits so we were researching.'

'And that's when we found the ghost.'

'Isn't that a bit . . . *intangible* . . . to be sold as a . . . well, as an item of consumer goods?'

'Well it doesn't come with a guarantee, of course.'

'No – you buy *something* – a jar or a garment or a picture . . .'

'And it's somehow steeped in *ghost* I suppose?'

'Justin, I don't think you're taking this seriously!'

'Well what did you want with a ghost anyway?'

'We didn't. We were just thinking that we might expand into that bit of the market – less work than packing up all those stakes – and Mary got a bit carried away and bid on one.'

'And won it!' Mary added triumphantly. 'Very reasonable.'

'It was a night-shirt – the actual object –

with a *very* nice letter attached, explaining that it had been found in an old wardrobe in a house *known* to be haunted. And we've definitely felt . . . vibrations in the ether, dear, haven't we?'

Auntie Mary nodded enthusiastically, and Justin recalled with regret his grandmother's Theosophist phase.

'But . . . well, it's difficult to be objective, Justin, and we really would like an outside opinion.'

'About getting your money back?'

'Well no – more about whether we really can claim we've got a ghost. So as you're staying overnight,' which Justin knew was unavoidable – it was a duty visit and he'd brought his toothbrush and pyjamas, 'we thought you might *wear* the night–shirt.'

As his tea went down the wrong way, Justin spluttered vehemently.

'I told you he wouldn't. Young people don't like old things.'

'Well we *did* wash it – not that it was *dirty* but Mary thought it smelled a bit iffy.'

'And that's another worry – have we washed the ghost away? We deliberately didn't use a pre-soaker . . .'

In the end it was, like most treaties composed under duress, an uncomfortable compromise. Justin would stay alone in the flat. There was only one bedroom (on his visits he usually occupied the sofa-bed in the living room), but his grandmother was adamant.

'It came with the night-shirt so I'm sure it's more of a bedroom ghost. I'll just stay overnight at your Auntie Mary's – she's got more space – so you'll have the place all to yourself.'

'With the ghost, of course!'

But his refusal to actually *wear* the night-shirt remained beyond negotiation.

After supper, when Maureen and Mary, buzzing with all the excitement of teens preparing for a sleepover, had left the flat, Justin registered his usual relief at being alone. He watched TV, worked a while on his laptop (studiously avoiding any visits to eBay), then went to bed with the edgy feeling of occupying an inappropriate personal space. This was his grandmother's room – there were frills and chintz and an old glass dressing table set of uncertain function. Much of the floor space, however, was occupied by something all too well known to him. Cardboard boxes had proliferated across the carpet, presumably in connection with eBay auctions won and items to be sold. *Like grandmother like . . .* thought Justin, who was similarly unable to throw away useful packing material.

Across the bed, the night-shirt had been neatly spread, arms out as though it was stretching luxuriously over the quilt. He had promised – oh yes, he really had promised – to leave it there while he slept. He sniffed it doubtfully, but got back only the faux-fresh smell of detergent. Well he would simply ignore it. Careful not to disrupt the garment, he wriggled delicately under the quilt and turned off the bedside lamp.

Letting his eyes adjust to the darkness he could see nothing amiss, just the jumble of boxes dimly lit by the illumination of a street light not quite quashed by the flowery curtain. Fine. Not too dark, not too light, not as chaotic as his own bedsit but not so worryingly empty as a faceless hotel room. Dutiful grandson humours dotty relation and is rewarded with enormous cooked breakfast. Wondering whether there would be black pudding, he settled down to sleep.

It was around 2.30am that he woke, with the immediate awareness that there was someone with him in the room.

Groping instinctively for the light switch, he heard himself saying, like a frightened child, 'Nanna? Nanna, is that you?'

Light – nothing, except the sense of being in the wrong room. He got up and padded to the kitchen for a drink of water. A searching look around – nothing. He went back to sleep.

By 5.30am he had drunk three glasses of water, been to the toilet twice (the two activities not being unconnected), had tried to distract himself with a household magazine, a cookery book and a knitting pattern and had decided that the first glimpse of morning light would see him up, dressed and drinking coffee. But it was still dark and he felt more tired than when he went to bed. It was the shirt, he decided, that was setting him off so.

Every time he saw its white scarecrow shape it must trigger his imagination, so that his fitful dozing was disturbed by the notion of a covert movement among the boxes, by a dim shadow thrown against the curtains, by something hesitant, something approaching but never touching him, something bending over to look into his sleeping face . . .

Right, that was it. He'd kept his promise but

enough was enough. He lifted the shirt from the bed, bundled it into a drawer full of unknowable old lady garments and settled under the quilt for the sleep he deserved, deep and comforting and undisturbed.

Then the *noise*, and he was fully awake.

Nothing. Yet for a moment he was sure one of the cardboard boxes had been pushed aside, with a sound no louder than an empty box shifted across a carpet, yet a sound nonetheless. Surely there *couldn't* be mice in this modern flat, upstairs . . . and no, it wasn't the scuttling of something small, so much as a *slide*, a push, a sense of something moved casually to make way . . . then he felt it. There was a pressure on the end of the bed.

In a second his mind was sorting rational options – old mattress, old bedstead, old springs springing the way that old springs sprung . . . No - *new* mattress, modern divan . . . Oh God – someone was sitting on the end of the bed!

He didn't dare turn on the light. To see might be worse than not to see, though the grainy brightness beginning to filter in through the curtains disclosed nothing. There *was* nothing, just a shifting of weight on a bed unused to his body and clearly much disturbed by his fitful night. There. It didn't feel like anything anymore. The mattress had settled and – no, oh God no! – the weight was shifting again, depressing the mattress closer to him.

Suddenly Justin felt the warmth of the quilt pressed closely against his knee – someone was touching his leg! Someone was sitting on the bed and touching his leg!

He leapt out from the other side of the bed and, pausing only to stub his toe on one of the boxes, reached the window and flung open the curtains.

Nothing – nada – no sign of a ghost, or a bed-shirt or even a rogue rodent. Just his grandmother's chintzy, untidy bedroom illumined by the light of early morning.

By the time the two women returned, bearing vacuum-packed bacon and a fresh loaf ('Don't really like those croissant things – they flake about everywhere'), Justin was up, washed, dressed and had mindlessly consumed a bowl of All-Bran as comfort food. Even so, his face told such a story that nobody needed to ask what sort of night he had spent.

Pausing for no longer than it took to brew a preliminary pot of tea, the old ladies sat down opposite him and demanded to hear the details.

Though Justin was not a natural story-teller, he could see that even *his* hesitant narration was winning smiles and nods of satisfied approval from his audience.

'There, dear,' said Mary when he had finished. 'That's sorted it all out *beautifully*. I'm so glad it's real and we can move into the ghost market – it was dreadfully heavy work, dragging all those stakes and mallets down to the Post Office. And we won't have to call on Mr Moorcock so often, which I know will put *your* mind at rest. I'll go and get the bacon started, shall I?'

Maureen waited until her friend had left the room. 'It's our new project, you see. We're going to cut up the haunted nightshirt into neat little squares and package them nicely for framing, so you can buy just a manageable relic, as you might say, of a genuine haunted garment. We just had to be sure . . .'

Justin felt his temper slipping. 'So that's why I had to be a guinea-pig – to vouch for the ghost!'

'Well it's Mary, you see. *I* say these things are all a matter of personal belief, but your auntie's *a bit of a Christian,'* she lowered her voice to suggest membership of some obscure cult, 'so she wasn't happy advertising anything as haunted if we hadn't given it a test-drive first.'

'But – you've been selling *vampire hunting kits,* for heaven's sake! Didn't you think *that* might be a tad fraudulent?'

His grandmother looked genuinely surprised at this lapse in logic.

'Of course not, dear. We didn't, after all, attempt to sell them *vampires*, just the kit. And I'm sure that if any of our satisfied customers *should* happen to meet a real vampire, our kits will work perfectly well. Mr Moorcock made those stakes out of some lovely old chair legs, and all the Holy Water came straight from the font at St. Botulph's – Mary used to collect it after they'd had a Christening.'

'So *will* people who buy the . . . the *bed-shirt patches* really get a ghost?'

His grandmother laughed. 'You slept in the same room as the shirt, *you* were haunted – we can say that with a perfectly clear conscience.'

'You set me up – it was all a trick! *You* made the noises and then... the . . . there wasn't a ghost at all!'

'Shhh dear – don't let Mary hear you say that! I've no idea whether the shirt is haunted, but

I know for a fact my bedroom is. That was just your grandfather you . . .' she hesitated slightly, '. . . were *aware of* last night. He's been turning up pretty regularly ever since the funeral. I thought that the sight of a strange man's shirt on the bed would definitely encourage a visit. He must have got quite a shock when he saw *you!* I don't doubt that he'll be back tonight to hear all about it.'

She paused. 'And that's why I'll be glad to see a little less of Mr Moorcock,' she said, wistfully. 'His attentions have been awfully flattering but you see I'm really not free. And he had been getting a little too close just lately, what with going so far as to offer me his toes . . .'

Auntie Mary poked her head round the door. 'Just getting breakfast ready now. Could you fancy a slice of black pudding?'

Gail-Nina Anderson *is older than the rocks whereon she sits. She has been a member of the Dracula Society since the 1970s, has spoken on the Undead everywhere from the Fortean Times Unconvention to Brompton Cemetery and is generally reckoned to be the world authority on the connections between vampirism and the Pre-Raphaelite Brotherhood. She lives in Newcastle, lectures on things art historical, organises the occasional exhibition and drinks unfeasible quantities of red wine. In her spare time she operates as an undercover agent for the Folklore Society, exploring the cult of the dreaded Vampire Rabbit of Old Newcastle Town.*

THE BOOK
Alan Brown

Once again I had arrived in the town centre far too early for my appointment. Being regularly let down by the local train service had prompted the habit of taking a much earlier train than necessary, resulting in having some time to kill. I had a number of plans for such eventualities. A walk by the riverfront, a visit to the arthouse cinema to pick up a list of forthcoming films or a browse in the only remaining bookshop the town centre had to offer.

This time it was the turn of the book shop so I found myself idly scanning the shelves in the occult/fantasy section. I did not have much hope of finding anything very interesting. I had a comprehensive collection of Lovecraft, Poe and the like and was not attracted by more explicit, modern fantasy novels and stories. My attention was attracted, however, by a quite slim, dark coloured paperback book which seemed somehow to give an impression of 'otherness' from the rest of the volumes. I could not explain this impression to myself but I felt this very strongly. At first sight, this book was different.

I picked up the book and looked at the cover, which was completely black except for the title and author picked out in silver lettering: 'Tales of the Blood' by Countess Dolingen. I had never heard of the writer and as I looked at the contents page I saw that this was a collection of short stories with a vampire theme to each one. Intriguingly, the back cover was blank, with no publishers 'blurb' to entice potential readers as is usually the case.

Realising I needed to get to my appointment, I made a quick decision to buy the book and headed to the cash desk. On the way I looked in vain for a price so I could get the money from my wallet. There was neither a printed price, nor a sticker from the shop. Hoping that I would not be charged an excessive amount I waited in the short queue at the counter.

The bored-looking assistant took the book and tried to find a bar code to scan into the computerised sales system. Not finding anything, she frowned and studied it more carefully for a price, or any clue at all as to what to charge me.

'I've never seen this before,' she said, and asked her colleague at the next till what she should do.

'Try putting the author or title into the computer and see what comes up,' was the suggestion. No information was forthcoming and, baffled by the system failure and exasperated at the lengthening queue behind me, the assistant finally agreed to charge me £5.99 for the book.

'It seems neither this book nor the author actually exist,' she said handing it to me. 'I don't know where we could have got it from!'

I did not get the chance to look at the book again until a few days later. I had a spare evening so sat down with a glass of wine in front of the fire to see what Countess Dolingen had to offer.

All the stories were of a similar, quite short length, around a dozen pages or so. Vampirism was the starting point for them all but this theme was interpreted in a different way each time. There was a tale about a lonely, divorced woman answering an advertisement in the personal column of a literary magazine. Having spent a couple of pleasant evenings with a charming, intelligent man in his early fifties, she agrees to go to his isolated country house so that he can cook her a special meal. Her suitor drugs the wine and she awakes to find herself chained to an elaborate funeral bier, having her blood gradually drained by her charming host.

Another story concerned the fate of a man whose car breaks down in the middle of nowhere and who is at first relieved to be picked up by a group of students returning from a night out. His relief is short lived as he comes to realise just what it is that his rescuers are studying. They are Satanists who have been looking for a suitable blood sacrifice to seal a contract with their dark lord.

The most disturbing of the eight or so stories in the book told of the activities of an extremely aged Church of England priest in his run down, almost unattended parish church in a decaying area of a northern industrial town. His novel way of providing the elements for Communion services was described by the author with peculiar relish.

While none of the stories were in themselves

particularly original or radical there was an undeniable strangeness about them, and the way they were written which reminded me of the first impression of 'otherness' I had when I first saw the volume on the bookshop shelf. Although in no way graphic, there was an air of genuine perversion lurking seemingly just off the page which left a haunting impression long after reading.

Over the next few days and weeks I found myself thinking about the book more often and wishing I could find out more about the mysterious Countess Dolingen, and perhaps find other works by her. I began to re-read the stories so often that I got to the point where I could quote whole sections to myself and indeed found myself doing this when I should have been concentrating on work or other more mundane matters. Finally, I became absolutely determined to trace the Countess and discover more of her writings, if there were any more to find. I decided to use my next holiday from work to do some serious research to this end.

All my efforts were in vain. Internet searches drew a blank whilst phone calls and visits to local libraries were equally unhelpful. Even the British Library web site and telephone enquiry service could not find a single scrap of information about the elusive Countess or her morbid literary output.

It was around this time that I began to notice a peculiar and disturbing change in my personality and general wellbeing. While I was engaged in my researches I felt fully alive, determined and full of energy. Yet when it came to all the other activities of life, such as work and socialising, I found it increasingly difficult to summon up any energy or enthusiasm. I abandoned friends, the house grew untidy and dirty, and I found myself neglecting regular meals and even personal hygiene. When my holiday period from work was over I phoned in to say I was sick and would not be returning until further notice. The only activity in which I had any interest was the increasingly baffling and frustrating search for Countess Dolingen, and with this I was becoming more and more obsessed.

My search then took a much darker and sinister turn. Considering the subject matter of the various 'Tales of the Blood', I began to explore via the internet a range of occult groups, starting in Britain, but when this proved fruitless, extending my researches to the rest of Europe. For a while I had the same lack of success. I came across a number of groups and societies both sinister and ludicrous.

But one day, whilst following up a Satanist group based in Belgium I finally had my first hint that the mysterious Countess Dolingen might actually exist. I found a reference to a cult of self-proclaimed vampires, established in the late 19th century in Bruges.

By following up and cross referencing a number of sources, including a letter kept in an archive by a Professor of Theology at a northern University, I finally had my first specific reference to a Count and Countess Dolingen who had lived in a canal side mansion in Bruges in the 1890s and who were rumoured to have had a daughter of considerable beauty, but highly sinister reputation. The vampire cult from that city had included this daughter in their ranks and she was considered to be a leading light in their repulsive activities. Whilst it was clear that this individual would now be long dead she may have had descendants to carry on the title. It was also possible that the vampire connection may now manifest itself in the writing of tales rather than the practice itself.

This finally seemed a potential breakthrough in my search so I arranged travel to Bruges and booked a week's accommodation in the Hotel Ter Brugghe. Prior to the journey I had found the name of a second-hand bookshop which some of the sources suggested may be a meeting place for the modern day successors to the 19th century occultists.

Accordingly, on my first full day in Bruges I made my way to this shop, located in a row of ancient properties on the bank of one of the smaller canals in a quiet part of the city. I was not sure how to pursue my search for the Countess from this point but intended to ask the proprietor if he knew of Countess Dolingen as a writer, and if he had any of her work.

When I arrived, however, the slightly odd-looking shop keeper was dealing with a customer, so whilst waiting I started browsing through the disordered piles of books on the various shelves. There did not seem to be any order to the volumes but I found myself strangely drawn to a case of books right at the back of the shop. Looking at the titles, I was both terrified and astonished to see a familiar plain, black volume exuding a sense of strangeness and otherness I had not felt since that fateful day a few months ago.

With a trembling hand I extracted the book. There was no mistake. The same plain back, the same silvery writing of the author and title –

'Tales of the Blood' by Countess Dolingen. I had of course brought my original copy with me and pulled this from my bag to compare the two. They were absolutely identical.

I was now alone in the shop with the proprietor. Unable at first to speak I simply showed him the book with a questioning expression on my face. I was sure that the man turned pale as he saw what it was I was showing him. Instead of speaking, he wrote something on a piece of paper, placed this and the book into a bag and gave it to me. I was not asked for any money and left the shop in a state of shock without saying a word.

I did not go straight back to the hotel but walked for a while, and then had a cup of coffee in a café. When I had recovered from the experience in the shop, I realised I had missed the opportunity to question the owner about the Countess to maybe find out how to contact her.

Remembering the piece of paper he had written on, I took this from the bag and saw, written in a spidery, shaky hand – 'The Chapel of the Holy Blood 6.00pm'. The Chapel is one of the most famous buildings in Bruges. It holds as a relic what is said to be a tiny amount of the blood of Jesus Christ, obtained at the Crucifixion and brought to the city following one of the crusades. Looking at my watch, I saw that it was now just after 3.00pm and I knew I could be in the Chapel at the time specified by the peculiar book seller.

It is strange how I had no doubts about any of this. Insane as it all seemed, I just knew that my search had led me quite deliberately to this point and that all of this was meant to happen. For the first time since I had bought 'Tales of the Blood' and begun my search for the author, I felt calm and composed. I waited serenely for the appointed time of 6.00pm with little more than a detached curiosity as to the outcome of the meeting I felt sure would finally happen.

I left my hotel for the short walk to the Chapel. I knew the way and did not want to arrive much before the appointed time. I had dressed, almost without realising it, in black clothes, as this seemed appropriate for both the location and the occasion.

The Chapel comprises most of one side of a large square with a set of carved steps in the corner of the square leading up to the entrance itself. At the bottom of the steps I saw a board giving times of services when the relic of the Holy Blood was brought out for veneration. There was such a service at 6.00pm.

I walked up the steps and into the Chapel. It was much smaller than suggested from the square outside, with no more than a dozen rows of high backed chairs. I gazed eagerly around but saw no one amongst the fifteen or so people seated who looked like the person I sought. It seemed to me that I would instinctively know when I saw the one I was fated to meet.

At exactly 6.00pm two priests entered through a door at the side of the altar. One was gently swinging a censor of incense and the other reverently carried an ornate silver box, evidently containing the Blood itself. All those present, including myself, stood as they walked to the altar. After a short prayer, the people were invited to come forward to venerate the relic.

I did not leave my place and, as the others were filing back to their places, I noticed for the first time, sitting at the back of the Chapel the figure of a woman dressed mostly in black with her face covered by a veil. Despite the veil, it seemed at that moment that our eyes met and the woman stood up and walked towards the Chapel exit. Without pausing for a moment to consider, I followed her down the carved steps and into the square.

There then followed a silent pursuit during which, whilst I never lost sight of the black clad figure, I was never able to come within more than twenty yards or so of her. We walked through many of the twisting, narrow streets of the city, avoiding those areas which would have been brightly lit and thronging with people. Even though it was still early in the evening it seemed we passed no one else at all during our strange procession.

We crossed over a number of canal bridges until I became convinced that we were going over the same ground more than once. Finally however, she led me into the part of the city near the last remaining active convent and down a narrow street that was not much more than a path. At the end of this there was a tall, darkened building, elegant but slightly decayed. Four steps led up to the door of the house and my guide paused and looked back towards me for the first time during our strange walk.

I could not see her face as she still wore her veil. Her glance was only momentary as she turned away and walked up the four steps. She seemed to enter the house without pausing to open the door and passed in silently. Without hesitation, but without unseemly haste, I followed her route up the steps and went in through the open door.

I could see virtually nothing of the interior as I walked in. There was almost complete darkness with just a faint almost phosphorescent glow near to the floor in front of me. It was as if the woman had left just enough of a trail of light to enable me to come to her without allowing me to see anything of her mysterious home. The faint glow led me on till I came to what seemed to be a large doorway or portal. The way was open and it seemed as I reached this point that the light increased just enough for me to read in letters carved over the doorway 'Countess Dolingen of Graz'. I walked ahead and for the first time was able to see my surroundings further than the floor just ahead of me.

I was in a large room, the ceiling of which was lost in the darkness above me. It was sparsely furnished; indeed, I saw only a single, large chair, so large in fact it was almost like a throne. Seated on this was the woman whom I had followed and who had led me to this fateful, inevitable meeting. I stopped a few yards from her, from a sense of awe, respect and a strange attraction.

She stood up and began to walk slowly towards me. She seemed to be of slightly below average height, slim, almost insubstantial. The only noise was a slight rustling of her long, dark dress brushing the floor as she moved toward me, almost gliding rather than walking. She was still veiled but, as she came within no more than a foot from me she stopped and, still without speaking, uncovered her face.

Her skin was very pale, the colour of milk, but stretched across the bones of her face with an effect that somehow suggested ancient parchment. Her age was somehow impossible to judge. Her bright red lips, accentuated by the pale skin, suggested youth and vigour but her remarkable eyes seemed old beyond reason, as if they had looked upon countless joys and sorrows that even the woman herself could not recall. It was a fascinating rather than a beautiful face, but a dark fascination, with as much about it to repel as to attract. We both stood looking at each other for what seemed an age until, finally, she spoke.

Her voice was quiet, so quiet I could only just hear the words with my ears though they resounded like cathedral bells in my mind. And this is what she said.

'I am Countess Dolingen. You have come to me through the Tales of the Blood. Only the one chosen by fate can ever find this book and thus be drawn to me. I have lived many life spans and must now renew my strength through you – the one chosen to renew the House of Dolingen. I will grow strong again through you and you will willingly give your blood to me, for this is your fate and your honour.'

As she spoke I felt no fear, only a growing realisation that what she said was true. I had been chosen by her and brought to her through the book. I would live on in her through all the ages of her immortal existence, sharing her passions, loves and hates. I would become one of the 'Tales of the Blood'.

Alan Brown *was born in Liverpool and is a retired Local Government officer. He first read* Dracula *aged 14. He lives in Bromborough in Wirral with his wife Cindy and their cats Puskas and Felix. He worked for Liverpool City Council for 36 years, plus spent 40 years as an Everton Football Club season ticket holder, which have both contributed to his knowledge of the un-dead. His main activities are being a house husband, increasingly bad football player and occasional food tester.*

A NIGHT TO REMEMBER
Jason D. Brawn

'You always play that song,' commented Geraldine Wright, as Shalamar's 1982 club smash, *A Night to Remember,* blared from the car speakers.

Her boyfriend, George Walker, explained, 'You know that this is my favourite song.'

'Yes, I know and you've told me before – it came out when you were born,' reminded Geraldine, already fed up with the song.

George was guiding his silver Porsche along through the dark woods of Epping Forest, passing through High Beech and making his way to Epping, where she lived. They were coming back from a night out at a multiplex cinema, in Edmonton, one of a few cinemas showing the latest Channing Tatum film, and she loved Johnny's Pizzas that was directly opposite.

A few rabbits whipped across the road, dodging speeding cars. Geraldine noticed and reminded George. 'Drive carefully. You don't want to hit them.'

'They're always out at this time of night,' he responded, lowering his speed. 'Sometimes, I've seen foxes get knocked over.'

His comment caused Geraldine to gasp. She loved animals and hated seeing them get hurt.

When the song finished, he quickly jabbed the replay button. Geraldine felt like protesting, but it was his car after all, and already it had been a wonderful evening with her fella. The headlights lit up the dark road ahead. It was getting late and Geraldine was already feeling tired.

Soon she managed to banish his music from her head, and only heard the soft drumming of the car engine. It was warm inside the vehicle and, along with the steady, soft, purring of the sound of the engine, and the scent of lavender air-freshener, she felt her eyelids beginning to droop. Geraldine leant her head back, while gazing out through the passenger side window. Just before sleep claimed her, she imagined there were dark shapes sitting in the trees lining the country road.

She began to dream that she was somewhere white and bright, with no walls or doors. Looking down, she saw that she was standing in a white mist, almost as if she were floating above clouds.

'Gel,' a dislocated voice whispered to her. Her name was repeated again, followed by someone shaking her shoulder. The white mistiness evaporated, darkness replacing it. 'Geraldine.'

She opened her eyes to see George's face, looking at her with concern.

'Do you want anything?' he asked politely.

Sitting up, she realised they'd stopped at a service garage. Bright, white light flooded through the windows, causing her to shield her eyes against it. She shook her head, leaning back in her seat once more.

'Won't be long,' he promised. A draught breezed in through his door as he climbed out, chilling her. George slammed it shut, the heat only slowly returning after he did so.

She watched him enter the shop, pace the long aisles looking for whatever it was he wanted. She guessed that he must be hungry and needed something to eat. She had watched him earlier, when he'd gulped down a large pizza and guzzled bottles of coca cola. It puzzled her why he was so skinny, but admired his larger than life personality. Geraldine loved his sense of humour, and after six weeks of dating she felt ready for the next stage.

George was still pacing up and down, browsing every aisle. *Come on. Come on.* Geraldine was beginning to lose patience: she needed to go home and catch some sleep before work tomorrow. 'Hurry up,' she murmured under her breath. Her eyes came to rest on the cash desk, and she noticed that there didn't appear to be anyone working behind the counter, which seemed rather odd.

Geraldine craned her neck, looking around to locate the attendant. *Maybe he's out the back,* she mused.

'What's keeping you,' she muttered under her breath, now beginning to feel stressed.

Without warning, all the lights inside and outside the service station went out.

'What the . . .' She jerked upright, straining to see what was going on. The shop was now in complete darkness. She waited for her eyes to adjust, hoped the lights would come back on soon. 'Don't do this to me.'

She whipped out her mobile and called

George's number. No answer. 'Come on, Georgie.' She hung up when it went through to voicemail. She stared out into the darkness, gulping nervously and fearing for the worst. The garage forecourt was in complete darkness and she felt totally alone.

Geraldine shrank from the idea of staying inside the car for the rest of the night, but what if George was in some kind of danger? After a moment of indecision about what best to do, she phoned 999 and waited. When the operator answered, Geraldine shakily told her, the words tumbling over one another, that her boyfriend could be in a hazardous situation, and that she was alone in a car. The female voice reassured her that a police car would be sent very soon.

Hearing that help was on its way, made Geraldine feel a little better. She cradled the phone in her hands, feeling its solid reassurance, her connection to the rest of the world. As extra insurance, she had also locked herself inside the car. Now it was just a question of waiting. The radio would have been good company at that moment, but without the ignition keys it wasn't going to happen. Instead, all she could hear was the wind whistling through the trees and the garage forecourt. When she looked back at the garage again, it appeared lifeless, like it had been abandoned for decades.

Time seemed to be slowing down. Her fear still took precedence over all other emotions, and soon her patience, never a strong point, had come to an end. Indecision again: stay in the car, where it was safe? Or go and see if she could find George? She was certainly in no mood for sleep, and George could be in danger or injured. If something had happened, surely he should have returned by now?

One, two, three . . . Geraldine steadied her nerves and opened the car door, feeling the bitter wind pounding on her face. She stepped out onto the tarmac, gently closing the car door, and gazed nervously at the remote service station. She walked over to the shop door, and pushed it quietly open. Inside it was dark, with only shafts of moonlight from outside faintly picking out shapes. The place smelled of floor-cleaner and something else: the sharp tang of fear. Her own fear.

When she looked out the garage forecourt, the area still looked deserted. The only sound she heard was the bitter wind whistling outside.

Moonlight guided her along the interior of the shop. She stepped carefully, slowly, not knowing what she might bump into but always dreading the worst. She moved as silently as she could, nervously, keeping her breathing as quiet as possible. Stopping for an instant to get her bearings, she heard muttering sounds about her. Unsure of where they were coming from, she cautiously kept going.

She turned a corner and saw, in the incidental light, perhaps half a dozen grey creatures – all with bald heads and pointed ears crouching in a corner, hunched over the bodies of George and the garage attendant. She could hear chewing and sucking noises. Nausea washed over her like a suffocating wave.

Stifling a scream, she turned and raced out of the lifeless service station, no longer caring about being quiet, desperate to get out.

The wind was much stronger now, whipping

her hair about her face as she fled across the forecourt. Suddenly four more of the monsters stood before her, blocking her path. When she let out a scream, they hissed in response, baring razor-sharp fangs exposed in fully gaping mouths.

All Geraldine could do now was to run towards the forest surrounding the service station. As soon as she made a break, the creatures took up the chase, snarling and yowling. She darted furiously, twigs and low branches whipping as she ran past. She dared not look behind her, not caring which way she was going or where it might lead. She just had to escape this nightmare; to survive, so that she could warn others.

Geraldine continued running, desperate to get away. Far, far away. Soon, the cries and howls became distant and, eventually, faded into silence. The only noise she heard was the sound of her own fleeting footfalls, thudding on the clear pathway which she hoped would lead to her safety.

Running out of breath, she slowed to a halt, finding herself completely lost. Her face tensed in panic, unable to work out where she was. Suddenly, she was alerted to the sound of a passing motor vehicle. She raced forward, forcing her way through the dense undergrowth of bushes and small trees, hearing only the sound of snapping branches and her own crunching footsteps.

She emerged onto a country road, and just caught sight of the rear of a passing police car. Geraldine frantically waved her arms for attention, but couldn't find the strength to chase her only saviour. She was breathless, but continued to gesture for the car to stop. It did, reversing around and lighting up her face with its headlights. Geraldine raised a 'thank you' grin and collapsed, exhausted, onto the road.

The squad car arrived to collect her. Two officers, one male and one female, both young, stepped out of the car to tend to Geraldine.

'There's nothing to worry about,' promised the female officer.

Geraldine gazed into her eyes, relieved and silent.

Sitting in the back seat of the police car, Geraldine stared glassy-eyed out of the window. Images of George's remains were all she could remember. Both officers were looking at each other, as if deciding what action to take next.

'Are you the one who called for help?' the female officer asked, turning in the front seat to look at Geraldine, who had plainly gone into shock. 'Do you have any injuries?' the policewoman asked calmly.

Still in shock, Geraldine didn't answer.

'Were there any casualties at the service station?'

The question jolted Geraldine out of her stupor, and she stared bewilderedly at the two officers. Her face crumpled and she burst into tears.

'Maybe we should check out the service station,' suggested the male officer.

'No! Please, no!' screamed Geraldine, lurching forward.

'In that case, we'll take you somewhere safe,' assured the policewoman.

Geraldine looked into her eyes, seeking reassurance from them. 'Thank you,' she whispered.

Geraldine sat back, aware of the squad car reversing and heading off in the opposite direction from the nightmare of the service station. Now, at last, she started to feel relaxed. The CB receiver spat out a welter of competing voices, announcing a police visit to the service station. The female officer immediately leant forward to switch it off, and both officers remained silent. But it disturbed Geraldine, who also leaned forward, and happened to see, at that moment, that the officer behind the wheel didn't cast a reflection in the mirror.

Geraldine's face grew rigid, as she stared with stunned silence. Her mouth opened, unable to speak. She was lost and didn't know what to do. Soon, the car picked up speed, tearing along the dark and windy road, taking her to some nightmarish destination. Her immediate thought was of a place, shrouded in blackness, where she could hear those revolting-looking creatures feasting on her. The thought of not being able to see them was almost more terrifying.

'I'm feeling sick,' started Geraldine in her choked voice. 'Please can you stop the car?' She continued pleading, but the car picked up more speed, frightening her more.

She watched the squad car make a few twists and turns, as if they were chasing someone. Geraldine tried to control her nerves.

'Please, I'm not feeling well?' she cried, hoping she could reason with them, but she sensed only their cold and primitive nature. She cried and yelled for mercy, but the officers refused to respond. Geraldine knew Epping Forest very well, but she didn't know where they were taking her.

Geraldine grasped at the door handle, desperate to open her door and fall out, but it was already locked. In response, a sheet of shatterproof glass quickly slid upwards, forming a partition between the driver and passenger that ensured Geraldine's capture.

The speed of the car kept increasing, and darkness was all she could see.

Eventually, the car began to slow down . . . and finally rolled to a halt.

A deathly silence surrounded her. Geraldine could see both officers sitting motionless, like waxwork figures. It was clear that she couldn't reason with them, and their personalities had changed from that of two responsible police officers to two . . . *vampires.*

For that's exactly what they were, as they slowly turned around and peeled off their masks, revealing themselves as grey creatures of the night. Immediately, the glass partition began to lower.

Jason D. Brawn *is the author of horror novelettes* Stranded *and* Refuge, *as well as having short stories, poems and film reviews published in anthologies, magazines and ezines. He has been a member of the Dracula Society for eight years. He resides in London and enjoys cinema, theatre, listening to obscure music, art, travelling and reading for inspiration.*

SANGUINE MEETS SANGUINARY
Rosemary Laurey

Success was so near, Abbott could taste it.

He waited in the shadows, slowing his breath, and forcing calm and purpose into every nerve ending. What a chance, to come upon Rooster, just like that. The bounty for Rooster's head – or any body part that would prove identity and demise - would cover every single debt Abbott had accumulated in his thirty-four years, provide for his old age and fund a nice little vacation in one of the leisure suburbs. The prospect warmed Jim Abbott's shriveled heart.

If only he were a few metres closer. He caught snatches of the conversation between Rooster and the two dealers. The cadence of the language was French, but Abbott couldn't understand the disjointed fragments drifting his way. He waited without moving, even when a bloated rat nibbled the toe of his boot. Feral rodents of all persuasions were part of the inner urban landscape; the gutters of rotting garbage attracted the four-footed sort, just as the Roosters of the world drew in the scum.

Scum that seemed as generous of their time as Rooster was of his money – or was it zip, or narco, or any one of the illegals that propped up the sagging economy of the innermost suburbs?

Abbott angled his neck for a better view. As the rat kept on gnawing, he envied Rooster's knee-high boots. Boots that no doubt concealed a number of knives – maybe even a self-destruct or two – and cost more than Abbott had earned in the past two months.

That was about to change. Hunters were paid by results and Abbott was about to pull in the big prize, and the right to loot the body: boots, fresh knives, and the black Anzo sidearms now resting in Rooster's belt. Not that Abbott would flaunt them like a hood.

With a final shake of hands and a last exchange in what sounded almost like French, Rooster and his two thugs parted. The duo slipped down an alley to the north and Rooster strolled off, so close to Abbott's hiding place he caught the glint of a wrist band as Rooster passed. It would be so easy to take him now but the hoods were still within earshot.

Giving Rooster time to get a safe distance ahead, Abbott slipped out of his dark doorway. At the corner, Rooster turned right. Abbott followed and went three paces before the stunner got him in the knees.

He fell, tasting blood as he stifled the scream, and crashed to the ground. He twisted, trying to ease the fire slashing his legs. As pain swelled to agony, Abbott groaned, not caring who saw or heard. What a way for a professional hunter to kick out? A bloody footpad's victim.

Abbott woke to soft, light, sweet-smelling sheets and the sensation of utter uselessness from his waist down. His feet and legs felt numb as dead snakes, his hips lay useless and his head throbbed but the air around was clean. A hospital? Unlikely. Rescue vehicles seldom braved the inner suburbs. But he was alive and, presumably, safe.

'You came to, I see.'

Abbott almost fainted. Rooster! It was a demented fever dream. Had to be.

A flesh and blood Rooster stood over him. 'I wondered how long you'd take to come to. They got you with a double stun. Those twins work in tandem.'

'Who?' None of this made sense.

'The Corsican twins. Were you following them, or me?'

'You,' he growled. Not much point in denying it.

Rooster chuckled. 'I thought so. They were convinced you were after them. Seems they share a very guilty conscience.'

'And you don't?' Hell! How many had Rooster killed, robbed, swindled, or nudged into the bondage of illegal substances? Rooster chuckled. Damned if Abbott could see what was so amusing.

'What the hell happened?'

'They zapped your kneecaps and left you for the rats to feed off.'

'And you took pity on me.'

'Not exactly. I had a use for you. They found

that amusing.'

He bet they did. Abbott's chest went cold. No use Rooster had for him could be anything other than painful. 'What did you do to me? I can't move!'

'I brought you here, removed your soiled clothes – very nasty they were after rolling in the gutter and that dark alcove wasn't much better – and since you appeared to be in extreme pain, I anesthetized your legs.'

'Made me helpless, you mean.'

'No, I blocked your pain.'

The man was sounding like a bloody philanthropist. 'Out of the kindness of your heart, I suppose.'

'Not in the least! I told you, I have a use for you.'

It was every hunter's nightmare to fall into the hands of the prey. And here he was, naked, immobile and disarmed.

'What do you want?' Might as well know up front. Or did he want to? The light in Rooster's eyes was enough to make anyone want to run.

Abbott shifted his upper body. His legs might be useless, but he still had two good arms. He moved again. Rooster didn't seem to notice. Just sat on the edge of the mattress, his weight tilting Abbott so he rolled towards him. A man would have to be blind not to notice the Anzo tucked in the wide belt. It was a wild hope, but if he could take out Rooster, and wait out the temporary paralysis . . . The odds were lousy, but current prospects were worse.

'Plan on starving me, do you?' Abbott feigned a light groan. 'Killing me slowly by thirst? Is a glass of water too much to ask?'

Rooster shrugged. 'Not in the least.' He rose. Abbott watched the dark thermo-plastic on Rooster's hip, gauging distance and opportunity. He took his chance, as Rooster turned.

An impossibly strong hand clamped down on his wrist. Abbott screamed as his bones grated.

'Hell no! You're too slow!' Rooster said, with a twisted grin. Dropping Abbott's throbbing hand on the covers, Rooster strolled over to the utility console in the corner and returned with a flask of water.

Abbott would have preferred it thrown in his face, but Rooster eased his arm behind Abbot's shoulders and raised his head, even tilting the cup to ease drinking.

Abbott's legs might be dead, but every nerve ending in his neck and back sensed the strength in Rooster's arm.

'Feeling better?' Rooster asked.

'No.'

'Sorry I can't offer you any food. I seldom have your sort visit.'

'Sorry to inconvenience you.'

The sarcasm was unacknowledged. 'No sweat. It's no great inconvenience since, as I said, I have a use for you,' he stood up to return the cup to the console. 'Two uses, in fact.'

If that was intended to instill fear, it worked. 'Only two? With your diverse interests?'

He acknowledged that with a shrug. 'Only two for you, Abbott. Hunters aren't that useful.'

'Not like pimps, pushers, killers and extortionists.'

A crease between his brows was Rooster's

only show of reaction. Baiting an assassin while immobile was probably unwise. So what? Abbott was dead meat already. It was just a matter of how long Rooster planned to drag it out.

'Get on with it!'

'Worried?'

'No. If I don't get you, they'll send someone else.'

'Most likely, but aren't you accorded one of the best?'

The compliment wasn't lost on Abbott. If the best could be so easily taken down... 'There are plenty of others.'

A lot of help worrying would be, but he did it anyway. While Abbott sweated though every pore that wasn't deadened, Rooster paced the small room. Stopping every few minutes to eye his captive, as if he were the latest in thermo-manufactured steak, or perhaps calculating how long he'd take to die. Abbott consoled himself with the fact that he'd spent the last bounty on a trip to the Caribbean enclaves. A man with no family or blood kin forfeited his estate to the government. That would be something to regret on his death bed.

'I do wonder,' Rooster said, after a long silence. 'What inspired your pursuit?'

Abbott's dry laugh broke the quiet. 'Three million Euroducats.' He'd have been set up for life.

Rooster acknowledged that with raised eyebrows and a slow whistle. 'That much, eh? Someone must love me . . . or not.'

'I think it's not.'

The smirk reappeared. 'I wouldn't argue with someone so closely aligned to the Gods of Security.'

Abbott couldn't hold back the chuckle. An apt description for the all-powerful chiefs of National Protection.

'They'll send someone else.'

'So you keep saying. I'd be disappointed if they didn't.' He turned and came closer. 'Meanwhile, you are here, so I must make the best of it.' He rested a long-fingered hand on Abbott's chest. 'Ever been bitten, Abbott?'

The light flash in Rooster's dark eyes was hideous confirmation of the truth behind the casual question.

'You're a bloodsucker!' cried Abbott.

'Now you can add 'vampire vermin' to my list of antisocial attributes.'

He was well and truly dead. Did anyone in Protection know this? Impossible. They'd never have sent him against a vamp. Or would they? If someone wanted him disposed of ...

Abbott, the renowned hunter, slain by a bloodsucker. That would be a tale. If they ever found him. Didn't victims desiccate? Or were they turned into vamps? That would be some end: a master hunter pursued by vermin disposal.

Rooster's hand felt like ice through the sheet. 'Relax. It won't hurt.' As if any fool would ever believe that. 'I regret imposing,'

Yeah right, thought Abbott. He hardly looked like a man, or rather, vamp, apologetic.

'But carrying you this far sapped my energy.'

'If it was that much effort, how come you didn't feed off me in the alley?'

'I said I needed you.'

Abbott tensed as Rooster picked up his arm. The room was cool, but that wasn't why Abbott was shivering. Hunters seldom died in their own beds, but he was about to die in a vampire's.

'If you were willing and cooperative, and your legs mobile, I'd take from the femoral artery. The sensation there is quite – specific – I've been told.'

'Your victims lived to tell?'

An almost-silver light glimmered in the vampire's eyes. He closed his cold fingers over Abbott's wrist and raised the hunter's arm over his head. Abbott tried to struggle, but as the light in Rooster's eyes burned brighter, it was as if every muscle and sinew in Abbott's body turned to mush. Too late, he remembered the folk wisdom about never meeting a vampire's eyes.

Rooster's lips brushed cold on the inside of Abbott's elbow. The bite seared. Heat flowed up Abbott's arm, like a boiling tide until his body was engulfed in warmth and yearning. His horror peaked with the awareness of one body part that wasn't, after all, paralyzed. His dick was hard. On the crest of his shock, came the pleasure: great waves of ecstasy that only compounded the horror. He was aware of his racing heart and heaving chest, as gasps of delighted agony, echoed round the silent room.

He was still panting minutes later, as Rooster pulled away and wiped his mouth with a towel, after licking Abbott's skin clean.

'That wasn't so bad, was it?' Rooster's eyes, and Abbott's, were on the still-rigid erection. 'Seems you enjoyed it in spite of yourself.'

'It was rape!'

'Of course it was.'

Rooster moved away and returned with another glass of water. 'Drink this, you need to replace the lost fluid.' Abbott gulped it down.

'Want more?' Rooster asked. Much as he hated to, Abbott nodded. The cool water eased the raging thirst. His raging erection was another matter.

Not that it bothered Rooster. He sat back down, thigh to thigh to Abbott. 'Thank you. That restored me.'

Abbott refused to say 'you're welcome'. Rooster wasn't.

'And now . . . I need a favour.'

'I don't do favours for vamps!'

Rooster ignored the interruption. 'I need you to give a message to Dermondy.' Dermondy? Abbott's director? What in …? 'Tell Dermondy: The seagulls are restless. Abort Wednesday.'

'What?'

'You heard. Simple enough, even for a hunter.'

'You think I'm here to deliver your messages?'

'Yes. As a way of thanking me.'

'Thanking you for what?'

Rooster's grin showed still-descended fangs tinged with blood. Abbott's blood. 'Thanking me, for not biting off your dick.'

Abbott let out a strangled scream. Rooster's hand circled his neck. All sound died as blackness engulfed him.

The ruddy birds woke him. Abbott did his best to ignore the dawn chorus but between the birds and the feral dog snuffling among the shrubs, it wasn't easy. He was alive. Most likely. He was pretty sure daffodils didn't grow in hell and stray dogs wouldn't cock their legs on your feet in heaven. In disgust, Abbott kicked the dog away and sat up in shock.

He wasn't paralyzed. Where he'd expected pain from demolished knees, he was fine. Had he dreamed last night? He looked down at his legs, encased in his own trousers and much cleaner than the last time he'd seen them.

He was dressed, uninjured, in what looked like an entertainment garden in one of the middle suburbs. His right arm ached inside the elbow, right where a livid bruise circled four neat punctures. Abbott wanted to vomit. It hadn't been a nightmare.

What now? He'd work out where he was and make for one of the bolt holes he maintained all over the city. As he stood, Abbott shoved his hands in his pockets. A stiff paper crinkled against his fingers.

He didn't want to read it but couldn't prevent himself.

'Remember to show your thanks.' It was written in large, open handwriting, signed with an overly ornate R.

Abbott all but ran to the nearest transstop. Less than an hour later, he was holed up behind a triple-locked door,

He waited three days, terrified of the coming change but he woke hungry for solid food every morning, and his teeth were just as crooked as ever. Hadn't Rooster infected him?

Apparently not. Relieved that he was still hunter and not vampire vermin. Abbott logged in to report.

'You're two days late, Abbott.' It was Smeigh, one of Abbott's most irritating contacts, but what the hell?

'I'm here. Got caught up with a cold trail. Thought I had Rooster but I missed him.' That was close enough to the facts to be acceptable. 'Anything new?'

'You missed some excitement.'

'What?'

'Shit hit the fan Wednesday night. Raid on an illegal Corsican warehouse. It was all set up, but they were waiting for us. We lost ten hunters and the police enforcers lost half a dozen.'

Abbott's hand closed around Rooster's note. 'Any of our section gone?'

'All ten were ours.' Half the section. 'Seems it was one of Dermondy's pet projects and he kept it in house.'

Abbott didn't remember signing off. He sagged on the end of the narrow bed, twisting Rooster's note between shaking fingers.

Maybe he'd be better off if Rooster *had* infected him.

***Rosemary Laurey** is a USA Today bestselling author. She is a retired special education teacher and grandmother who now lives in Ohio and has a wonderful time writing and letting her imagination run riot. As Rosemary, she writes paranormal and contemporary romance. Her work has received numerous nominations and awards including the PRISM Best of the Best and the Dorothy Parker Award. For news of Rosemary's latest releases, her website can be found at www.rosemarylaurey.com.*

SCRUFFY THE VAMPIRE SLAYER

Tina Rath

Scruffy dressed carefully for the first day of her new term at St. Walburga's. She wanted to strike a balance between looking too cool, and so attracting the unwelcome attentions of the Griswold Gang, who did not believe in people getting ideas above their station, and looking too geeky, which would simply make her a target for everyone else.

Scruffy was not, in fact, particularly worried by bullies. Her policy of hitting out and hitting hard when attacked usually stood her in good stead. Still, there was no need to borrow trouble. With this in mind she darted through the dreary concrete exercise-yard in front of St. Walburga's, where the Griswold gang were lolling about, comparing designer labels, swapping the names of their probation officers, re-forging alliances, re-igniting feuds and extracting the lunch money from the small and weak, and made briskly for the school library.

The Griswold gang would never be found in

the library. Many of them probably did not even know where it was. Some of them were convinced that the whole literacy thing was a giant con-trick: people just pretended to find some meaning in those intricate patterns they called letters specifically to annoy the Griswolds. Others were prepared to concede that reading was possible, though not necessarily desirable, but it was less a learned skill than a trick, which they had somehow missed being shown – perhaps they were playing truant on the day the class did it.

Scruffy slipped into the room and realised at once that something was different. Not the books themselves, certainly. They still looked like a collection of jumble sale rejects waiting for the bin men in a Nissen hut. Not the furniture, not . . . Scruffy gave a little squeak as she realised that she was being watched. Someone was sitting at the Librarian's desk.

Her first thought that he was very good-looking, not in the pretty-boy-band way that she admired herself, but in the haggardly-handsome style her mother preferred. Indeed, for a moment, she thought she might have seen him on the telly – in a commercial, perhaps? But no – telly people, unless they were reporters looking for sound bites on inner city decay, the failure of the government's education policy, or teenage immorality – were not likely to turn up at St. Walburga's. Then she realised that she was staring at him, but it hardly mattered because he was staring at her as well.

'Scruffy?' he said, uncertainly. 'Are you – er – Scruffy?'

He had the kind of accent that the Griswolds automatically associated with sexual deviation, but Scruffy's Nan, an unreconstructed East Ender, would have called him a gentleman.

'Yeah,' said Scruffy, adding automatically, 'I didn't do anything. We're allowed in here.'

'Yes, I know. I've been waiting for you. I'm your Watcher.'

'And just what,' Scruffy demanded, her eyes narrowing, 'did you want to watch me doing?' She had heard about middle-aged men like this, but it was the first time she had actually met one.

'No, no, I mean – do you know what a mentor is?'

Here she was on safe ground. She had seen them in the *Narnia* films. 'It's a half-man, half-horse, but . . .'

The new librarian sighed. You got the feeling that he was beginning to realise that things were going to be a lot more difficult than even he had bargained for . . .

Scruffy huddled in the shadow of a flying buttress attached to the Gothic, soot-stained walls of St Elphege's church, trying to psych herself up to making her first patrol in her capacity as Vampire Slayer.

She had eventually accepted that Mr Harris the Librarian was for real and that she really was the Chosen One, the one frail bulwark between St. Walburga's and its environs and the minions of Hell. She was also, unconsciously, acquiring a good deal of Mr Harris' vocabulary.

Only a few weeks ago she would not have known what bulwarks, environs or minions were – well, she might have made a stab at bulwarks, but she would have been wrong. She was yet to see a vampire, but she believed, partly because it was the only way to explain the presence of Mr Harris (MA, Ph.D Cantab) in St Walburga's library. Only some kind of supernatural intervention (or a really terrible crime in a previous life) would have placed a classics specialist there.

And if it *was* all true, Mr Harris: Watcher, Scruffy: Slayer, it meant that somewhere in the litter infested buddleia jungle that was St. Elphege's churchyard lurked her legitimate pointy toothed prey. In spite of her crash-course in unarmed combat, plus the use of club, sword, crossbow and stake, she was by no means certain that she was really going to be able to deal with them.

Her main problem, even before the questions raised by the semi-immortality and superhuman strength of her opponents, was 'What if I get it wrong, and try to stick a pointy piece of wood through a perfectly innocent civilian?' Quite apart from the embarrassment, might it not lead to a prison sentence? Mr Harris had been less than reassuring: well, he had insisted that she would always recognise a vampire. It came with the territory. If she met one, saw one, even heard or smelt one, she would know. And were she to make a mistake then they certainly wouldn't send her to prison.

'Much more likely to remand you in custody for a medical report,' he had added, rather spoiling the effect.

Well. There was only one way to find out. She stepped out of her shelter and began her patrol.

There was a full moon, but this hardly

mattered. The church-yard was permanently lit by the sodium lamp stands which lined the streets beyond, making it look like a sunny day in Hell. But even their light could not penetrate the deep dark shadowy places . . . and it was into these shadows that she would have to go.

She took a deep breath, stepped forward and tripped over a fallen grave stone, landing in a heap of unspeakable litter. She yelped, swore, massaged a grazed shin . . . and stayed on the ground.

Just ahead of her she could hear a murmur of conversation. A man and a woman were talking. *Oh, right,* she thought, *a couple looking for somewhere quiet – or a working girl and her client, agreeing terms. They'll think I'm a Peeping Tom.* But . . . something in the sound of one of those voices raised the hairs on the back of her neck. Just as Mr Harris had said. She knew deep in her bones. One of the voices was human. The other, she was fairly certain . . . was not. Only a few metres away someone was being chatted up by a vampire.

She crept closer. Beyond the shadows was a little patch of open ground. A big boxy sort of tomb thing stood in the middle, and on the tomb sat a lady, in lacy Victorian gear, holding a sketch pad. Talking to a Vicar. Scruffy could clearly see his white dog collar gleaming in the moonlight. Right. Or rather, not right. Because according to her finely-honed Slayer senses the lady was human and the Vicar was a vamp.

For two vital seconds she hesitated, not really trusting herself. And then there was a sudden ugly eruption of teeth and the Vicar was lunging at his victim's jugular. Scruffy sprang forward, stake held in the approved jabbing position. She might have been too late even so, but the lady dropped her sketch book and pulled a silver cross from under her high-collared blouse. It might not have proved a permanent solution, but it kept the vampire off for just long enough to give Scruffy a chance to jab her stake under his short ribs (Slayer Manual fig.3). Mercifully, instead of turning on her with the roar of an outraged Anglican cleric, he exploded in a cloud of dust.

'Well done, er – Scruffy,' said Mr Harris, emerging from the buddleia. Scruffy realised that he must have been following her on her first patrol and wondered if she should feel touched or cross.

'Ah – er – good evening?' he added, turning to her rescuee. Even at this moment Scruffy could admire the way he could make a conventional greeting sound like 'and what the . . . are you doing here?'

The lady stood up. Her lacy blouse and long flounced skirt were black (and slightly ragged when viewed close to) so Scruffy assumed that she was a somewhat elderly Goth. The sketch book which lay on the ground between them showed a more than competent pencil drawing of St. Elphege's church by moonlight.

'I'm Saffron,' she said cheerfully. 'Sorry about that, but my parents were hippies. I'm a freelance artist, and I've been asked to come up with some suggestions for a cover for a paperback collection of horror stories. I thought I'd start with a few sketches of St. Elphege's and – rather foolishly I suppose, I wanted to catch it by moonlight –'

'And why you have remained so completely unperturbed by this vampire attack?' said Mr

Harris.

'Ah – well, I was wondering if something of that sort might happen. I really *am* a freelance artist, but I'm also – involved with a sort of New Age Group. I've been sent here by my Chapter to check out some rather ominous signs –'

'Like that?' Mr Harris asked, looking at the little heap of dust, surmounted, incongruously, by a clerical collar which was all that remained of the Vampire Vicar.

'Well, that as well – but we've checked the omens very carefully, and they suggest that you're sitting on a Hell Mouth.'

Mr Harris ran a hand through his already romantically tousled hair. 'What a surprise!' he said wearily.

'Which is due to blow at any moment,' Saffron continued. 'Probably on Halloween, Hell being kind of traditional. When Hell will, quite literally break loose and take over.'

Mr Harris looked round at the desecrated churchyard, lit by the stark sodium glare. 'And when it happens,' he said, 'how will we tell?'

It was Scruffy's mum's proudest boast that she had always been 'there' for her daughter. More specifically she had been there with a nice cooked tea every evening on Scruffy's return from school.

This state of affairs was achieved by her insistence on accepting only lunchtime engagements as an exotic dancer at such local venues as *The Dog and Ferret*, or *The Marlborough Arms*, with an occasional special evening performance contrived by enlisting the assistance of Scruffy's Nan as a sitter, at such times as she was not pursuing her own vocation as life model and Character Extra, but now that her daughter had reached the years of discretion, Scruffy's mum had decided to devote more energy to her own career, after all, as she informed her daughter almost tearfully, she only had a few years left before she joined Nan on the Ugly Register. With this in view, she had obtained an engagement as a table dancer at the House of Atreus Burger Bar and Grill Palace, a newly opened eating establishment of unusual opulence run by the handsome and charismatic Mr Atreides.

So Scruffy's mum now spent her evenings gyrating to loud music, while wearing a red PVC bikini, glittery horns and matching tail, all of which, except the horns, were readily detachable when required.

It must be said that Scruffy's mum was quite as stern an upholder of the 'Look, Don't Touch' rule as was Mr Atreides himself who, jealous for his licence, patrolled his territory as nervously and regularly as Scruffy did hers, watching with simple pleasure when Scruffy's mum enforced his rules, if necessary, with that splendid right hook she had passed on to her daughter. Indeed, he seemed to take so much pleasure in watching her that her colleagues had begun to make jokes about love and even weddings which, Scruffy's mum maintained – with only a slight trace of wistfulness – was as likely as her appearing for her performance in full wedding dress and veil . . .

So there was no question of her interfering

with Scruffy's patrols, or with the long hours she spent in the library helping, or at least attempting to help Mr Harris and Mrs Walden (as Saffron, for some reason beyond Scruffy's comprehension, liked to be known) in their increasingly desperate attempts to find a way of capping the Hell Mouth. She could at least make coffee and do odd bits of photocopying when she was not staking vampires, and punching out demons.

There had been a moment when they thought they had cracked it. Mr Harris found a reference in an obscure document to a method of capping the Hell Mouth by filling it with 'creatures moore eevil than thoose which essay to issue foorth.' But there was no indication as to where these creatures might be found, and further research revealed that the author had been, in Mr Harris's unhappy opinion, 'as mad as a box of frogs.'

Time passed and no discoveries were made. Indeed the day came when Scruffy realised that St Walburga's Halloween Disco was scheduled for that very afternoon (no one was uncool enough to come to school in the evening) and there had been no breakthrough. Scruffy listlessly turned out a shiny red leotard, found some red tights, borrowed a spare pair of her mother's horns and set off for school. Before going to the pumpkin infested gym she paid a brief visit to Mr Harris, and found him deeply depressed, brooding over a pile of Latin primers.

'All I ever wanted to do was to teach Latin, you know,' he told her. 'And for all the good I've done as a Watcher, they might as well have left me to it.'

'You couldn't have been a better Watcher,' said Scruffy, then, realising this sounded rather final, she added, 'maybe Saffron's got it wrong.'

'No, she's right. All the signs are here'. He looked up and caught sight of the horns. 'Have you adopted protective colouration?

'Nah. I thought I ought to go to the disco. I mean, if anything is going to erupt, it will probably be there.'

'Again,' he said bitterly, 'how will you tell?'

On her arrival in the gym, Scruffy saw what he meant. A blasphemous heavy metal track blasted from the sound system. Someone had already spiked the fruit punch, probably not just with alcohol. Scenes that would not be out of place in the suppressed outtakes from the film *Caligula* were taking place under the fixed glares of paper pumpkins. Teachers seemed to be acting on the principle of joining those they were unable – in any sense of the word – to beat. For a moment Scruffy wondered if Hell was indeed erupting right there.

And then there was an unearthly cry from the corridor, a cry that overrode even the Blood Beasts' rendition of *Slaughterfest Five.* Saffron was screaming – not calling for help, just screaming on one horrible, mad banshee note. Without hesitation Scruffy turned and pelted out of the gym. Unfortunately so did the greater part of the Griswold gang, bored already with simple depravity, and looking for stronger meat. Nevertheless she arrived ahead of them in the Library, and there she realised that she had been wrong. Hell was not about to erupt in the gym. It was erupting already in the reference section of the library.

Horrors in shapes so *wrong* that they hurt the eyes were boiling out of the floor. And one of them had wound a disgusting tentacle around Saffron. She was still screaming, so Scruffy supposed she was still alive. Mr Harris having thrown his Latin primers at the monster without noticeable effect was now jabbing at it with a pair of dividers.

Scruffy dived forward, attacking the tentacle with fists and feet. The touch of it made her feel sick, but that hardly seemed to matter.

'Drop her!' Scruffy shrieked. 'I'm the Slayer! Leave her! Take me!'

Mr Harris was trying to push her aside, protesting that if Hell was going to cherry pick victims then he was the obvious choice . . . and the tentacle wavered. It was clearly not prepared to have victims struggling to throw themselves into his (its?) clutches. It wanted to grasp this unexpected bounty, but Hell Mouth was not yet wide enough to get another tentacle through. To gather in Scruffy and her Watcher, it (she?) would have to release Saffron, if only for a moment. That momentary waver was enough to allow Mr Harris and Scruffy to wrench Saffron free and drag her back to the Librarian's desk.

And then the entire Griswold gang piled into the room.

'Reinforcements for Hell Mouth!' Saffron moaned.

'Possibly not . . .' said Mr Harris, a note of hope suddenly infiltrating his habitual tone of gloom.

There was a moment of stasis as Horrors met Griswolds. The front ranks of Hell, who could see (sense?) what was coming, came to a halt. There was some evidence of a scrimmage behind them.

'But those behind cried 'Forward', and those before cried 'Back',' murmured Mr Harris.

The Griswolds, perhaps moved by simple curiosity, perhaps recognising kindred – Things – moved forward. And the Horrors fled back with eldritch cries which could very probably be translated as '. . . this for a game of toy soldiers. I'm off!' as the Griswolds flocked after them . . . and Hell Mouth snapped shut. All that remained in the library were Saffron, Mr Harris, Scruffy, a scattering of the young and innocent who had been drawn after the Griswolds in the stampede from the gym, and a faint smell of sulphur.

One of the first year pupils, too young to have been fully inoculated with the St Walburga ethos, began, helpfully, to gather up the spilled pile of books.

'Are these yours, sir?' she enquired.

'Eh? Oh, yes. Latin books . . .'

'Latin?' Several of the other first years peered over her shoulder.

Somehow, suddenly, they were sitting in a circle on the floor, with Latin primers on their knees. Saffron was briskly photocopying the opening pages for those who did not have their own book.

Somewhere, so far underground that it must have been in another dimension, there were strange sounds, sounds suggesting that . . . Things . . . were thrusting unimaginable articles into trunks and suitcases of shapes that defied earthly geometry, coaxing small tentacled monstrosities into pet-carriers of no mundane design, putting larger tentacled monstrosities into warm coats, and hurrying them out to unearthly vehicles, calling to each other to make sure that Auntie R'kshesta had got a lift, and that little Yog-S'bash had taken his travel-sickness pills . . . sounds in other words suggesting that the original inhabitants of Hell Mouth were moving out as fast as possible to a more desirable location. But neither Mr Harris, nor his Latin class, paid any attention.

'Discipulis picturam spectate,' said Mr Harris. 'Now, look at the first word. What English word does it remind you of?'

'Disciples!' shrieked Caleb, who was excused religious instruction because his parents belonged to the small and rather obscure sect, the Church of Universal Damnation, and who, therefore, knew the Bible, and Biblical language, rather

'Quite right. And what are disciples?'

'Followers,' said Caleb confidently. 'People who follow –'

'And learn, perhaps?'

Caleb nodded

'So in this context perhaps we can translate this as 'pupils' or 'students'.'

'Us!'

'Quite right. Now, 'picturam' is, of course, easy.'

'Picture!' roared his class.

'Students, look at the picture!' yelled Said, romping ahead.

They had translated their first Latin

sentence.

'Is it all as easy as that?' Kyeleigh demanded.

'No,' said Mr Harris firmly. 'Some of it is very difficult indeed.'

They settled down happily. It was the first time that anyone had suggested that they were capable of difficult work. Scruffy, who had already been introduced to the concept, smiled wryly.

'Made the world safe for Latin lessons, then, have we?'

'For the time being – and with the unwitting help of the Griswold gang,' said Mr Harris. For a moment his haggardly handsome face looked just haggard. And then, as he looked back at his pupils it softened again and he looked almost young and hopeful. 'Would you like to join us?'

Scruffy hesitated for a moment, then sat down. She had learned how to kill vampires. Latin should be a doddle. Saffron offered her some photocopied pages, and Scruffy noticed that her black blouse and skirt was now as white as a wedding dress, the ragged edges transformed to delicate lace. And as for herself she saw, with only mild curiosity that her devil costume had mutated into a very pretty bridesmaid's dress.

She took a moment to wonder if the same sort of thing had happened to her mother, before turning her attention to a map of the Roman Empire.

Tina Rath *lives in London and works - when she can - as an actress, model and Queen Victoria look-alike. Her stories have been published in the* *small and mainstream press, and she has several novels looking for publishers. She is also a vampire expert who has appeared in a number of documentaries, and recently wrote an extended introduction to the David & Charles e-book of* Dracula, *available on Amazon, as is her collection of short stories,* A Chimaera in My Wardrobe. *A new and startling website is under construction but meanwhile further information can be found on www.academicvampire.co.uk.*

Made in the USA
Lexington, KY
10 May 2015